D0209384

Book 12

CIRQUE DU FREAK
THE SAGA OF DARREN SHAN

Sons of Destiny

Book 12

CIRQUE DU FREAK

THE SAGA OF DARREN SHAN

Sons of Destiny

by Darren Shan

LITTLE, BROWN AND COMPANY

New York ∽ Boston

Copyright © 2006 by Darren Shan

All rights reserved. Except as permitted under the U.S. Copyright Act of 1976,
no part of this publication may be reproduced, distributed, or transmitted in any
form or by any means, or stored in a database or retrieval system, without the
prior written permission of the publisher.

Little, Brown and Company

Hachette Book Group USA
237 Park Avenue, New York, NY 10017
Visit our Web site at www.lb-teens.com

First U.S. Edition: September 2006

First published in Great Britain by Collins in 2004.

The characters and events portrayed in this book are fictitious.
Any similarity to real persons, living or dead, is coincidental
and not intended by the author.

Library of Congress Cataloging-in-Publication Data

Shan, Darren.
Sons of destiny / by Darren Shan. — 1st U.S. ed.
p. cm. — (The saga of Darren Shan ; bk. 12)
Summary: As Darren faces the final showdown with his archenemy, Steve
Leopard, he seeks a way to trick destiny and avoid the requirement that one of
them die and the other become Lord of the Shadows, fated to destroy the world.
ISBN-13: 978-0-316-15629-5 (hardcover)
ISBN-10: 0-316-15629-9 (hardcover)
[1. Vampires — Fiction. 2. Fate and fatalism — Fiction. 3. Horror stories.]
I. Title: At head of title: Cirque Du Freak. II. Title.

PZ7.S52823Son 2006
[Fic] — dc22
2005057894

10   9   8   7   6   5   4   3   2

Q-FF

For:

Bas, Biddy, and Liam — my three pillars

OBEs
(Order of the Bloody Entrails) to:

"Lucky" Aleta Moriarty

A and Bo — Bangkok's best banshees
Emily "Lilliputian" Chuang
Jennifer "Stacey" Abbots

Saga Editors:
Domenica De Rosa, Gillie Russell, Zoë Clarke, and
Julia Bruce — you done good, girls!!!

Bloody Brilliant Buccaneers:
The Christopher Little Cutthroats

And an extra special thank-you to all of my Shansters,
especially those who have kept me company on Shanville.
Even in death may you all be triumphant!

Also in the CIRQUE DU FREAK series:

PROLOGUE

IF MY LIFE WAS a fairy tale and I was writing a book about it, I'd start with, "Once upon a time there were two boys called Darren and Steve. . . ." But my life's a horror story, so if I were to write about it, I'd have to begin with something like this instead:

Evil has a name — Steve Leopard.

He was born Steve Leonard, but to his friends (yes — he had friends once!) he was always Steve Leopard. He was never happy at home, didn't have a dad, didn't like his mom. He dreamed of power and glory. He yearned for strength and respect, and time in which to enjoy it. He wanted to be a vampire.

His chance came when he spotted a creature of the night, Larten Crepsley, performing in the wondrous magical show, the Cirque Du Freak. He asked Mr. Crepsley to blood him. The vampire refused — he said Steve had bad blood. Steve hated him for that and vowed to track him down and kill him when he grew up.

Some years later, as Steve was preparing for his life as a vampire hunter, he learned about the purple-skinned, red-eyed vampaneze. In legends, vampires are wicked killers who suck humans dry. That's hysterical garbage — they only take small amounts of blood when they feed, causing no harm. But the vampaneze are different. They broke away from the vampire clan six hundred years ago. They live by laws of their own. They believe it's shameful to drink from a human without killing. They always murder when they feed. Steve's sort of people!

Steve went in search of the vampaneze, certain they'd accept him. He probably thought they were as twisted as he was. But he got it wrong. Although the vampaneze were killers, they weren't inherently evil. They didn't torture humans, and they tried not to interfere with vampires. They went about their business quietly and calmly, keeping a lower-than-low profile.

I don't know this for sure, but I'm guessing the vampaneze rejected Steve, just like Mr. Crepsley did. The vampaneze live by even stricter, more traditional rules than vampires. I can't see them accepting a human into their ranks if they knew he was going to turn out bad.

But Steve found a way in, thanks to that eternal

agent of chaos — Desmond Tiny. Most just call him Mr. Tiny, but if you shorten his first name and put it with his last name, you get Mr. *Destiny*. He's the most powerful person in the world, immortal as far as anyone knows, a meddler of the highest order. He gave the vampaneze a present many centuries earlier, a coffin that filled with fire whenever a person lay within it, burning them to ashes within seconds. But he said that one night someone would lie in the coffin and emerge unharmed. That person would be the Lord of the Vampaneze and had to be obeyed by every member of the clan. If they accepted this Lord, they'd gain more power than they'd ever imagined. Otherwise they'd be destroyed.

The promise of such power proved too much for Steve to ignore. He decided to take the test. He probably figured he had nothing to lose. He entered the coffin, the flames engulfed him, and a minute later he stepped out unburned. Suddenly, everything changed. He had an army of vampaneze at his command, willing to give their lives for him and do anything he asked. He no longer had to settle for killing Mr. Crepsley — he could wipe out the entire vampire clan!

But Mr. Tiny didn't want the vampaneze to crush the vampires too easily. He thrives on suffering and conflict. A quick, assured victory wouldn't provide him with enough entertainment. So he gave the vampires a get-out clause. Three of them had the ability to kill the Vampaneze Lord before he came fully into his powers. They'd have four chances. If they were successful and killed him, the vampires would win the War of the Scars (that's what the battle between the vampires and vampaneze was known as). If they failed, two would die during the hunt, while the third would survive to witness the downfall of the clan.

Mr. Crepsley was one of the hunters. A Vampire Prince, Vancha March, was another. The last was also a Prince, the youngest ever, a half-vampire called Darren Shan — and that's where I come in.

I was Steve's best friend when we were kids. We went to the Cirque Du Freak together, and through Steve I learned of the existence of vampires and was sucked into their world. I was blooded by Mr. Crepsley and served as his assistant. Under his guidance I studied the ways of vampires and traveled to Vampire Mountain. There I undertook my Trials of Initiation — and failed. Fearing death, I fled, but during my escape I uncovered a plot to destroy the clan. Later I exposed it, and as a reward I was not only accepted into the fold, but made a Vampire Prince.

After six years in Vampire Mountain, Mr. Tiny set me on the trail of the Lord of the Vampaneze, along with Mr. Crepsley and Vancha. One of Mr. Tiny's Little People traveled with us. His name was Harkat Mulds. Little People are grey-skinned, stitched-together, short, with large green eyes, no nose, and ears sewn beneath the flesh of their heads. They're created from the remains of dead people. Harkat didn't know who he used to be, but we later found out he was Kurda Smahlt in his previous life — the vampire who'd betrayed the clan in the hope of preventing the War of the Scars.

Not knowing who the Vampaneze Lord was, we missed our first chance to kill him when Vancha let him escape, because he was under the protection of Vancha's vampaneze brother, Gannen Harst. Later, in the city of Mr. Crepsley's youth, I ran into Steve again. He told me he was a vampaneze hunter and, fool that I was, I believed him. The others did too, although Mr. Crepsley was suspicious. He sensed something wrong, but I convinced him to grant Steve the benefit of the doubt. I've made some terrible mistakes in my life, but that was certainly the worst.

When Steve revealed his true colors, we fought, and twice we had the power to kill him. The first time we let him live because he wanted to trade his life for Debbie Hemlock's — my human girlfriend. The second time, Mr. Crepsley fought Steve, Gannen Harst, and an impostor, who was pretending to be the Lord of the Vampaneze. Mr. Crepsley killed the impostor, but then was knocked into a pit of stakes by Steve. He could have taken Steve down with him, but let him live so that Gannen and the other vampaneze would spare the lives of his friends. It was only afterward that Steve revealed the truth about himself, and made the bitter loss of Mr. Crepsley all the more unbearable.

There was a long gap between that and our next encounter. I went with Harkat to find out the truth about his past, to a waste world full of monsters and mutants, which we later discovered was Earth in the future. Upon my return I spent a couple of years traveling with the Cirque Du Freak, waiting for destiny (or Des Tiny) to pit Steve and me together again for one final clash.

Our paths finally crossed in our old hometown. I'd returned with the Cirque Du Freak. It was strange revisiting the past, walking the streets of the town where I'd grown up. I saw my sister Annie, now a grown woman with a child of her own, and I ran into an old friend, Tommy Jones, who'd become a professional soccer player. I went to watch Tommy play in an important international game. His team won, but their celebrations were cut short when two of Steve's henchmen invaded the pitch and killed a lot of people, including Tommy.

I chased after the murderous pair, straight into a trap. I faced Steve again. He had a child called Darius with him — his son. Darius shot me. Steve could have finished me off, but didn't. It wasn't the destined time. My end (or his) would only come when I faced him with Vancha by my side.

Crawling through the streets, I was rescued by a pair of tramps. They'd been recruited by Debbie and an ex-police inspector, Alice Burgess, who were building a human army to help the vampires. Vancha March linked up with me while I was recovering. With the ladies and Harkat, we returned to the Cirque Du Freak. We discussed the future with Mr. Tall, the owner of the circus. He told us that no matter who won the war, an evil dictator known as the Lord of the Shadows would rise to rule and destroy the world.

As we were trying to come to terms with the shocking news, two of Steve's crazed followers struck — R.V. and Morgan James, the pair who'd killed Tommy. With the help of Darius, they slaughtered Mr. Tall and took a hostage — a young boy called Shancus. Half human, half snake, he was the son of one of my best friends, Evra Von.

As Mr. Tall lay dying, Mr. Tiny and a witch called Evanna mysteriously appeared out of nowhere. It turned out that Mr. Tiny was Mr. Tall's father, and Evanna his sister. Mr. Tiny stayed to mourn the death of his son, while Evanna followed us as we chased after her brother's killers. We managed to kill Morgan James and capture Darius. As the others hurried after R.V. and Shancus, I stole a few words with Evanna. The witch had the ability to see into the future, and she revealed that if I killed Steve, I would take his place as the dreaded Lord of the Shadows. I'd become a monster, murder Vancha and anybody else who got in my way, and destroy not just the vampaneze, but humanity as well.

As shocked as I was, there was no time to brood. With my allies, we tracked R.V. to the old cinema where Steve and I had first met Mr. Crepsley. Steve was waiting for us, safe on the stage, separated from us by a pit that he had dug and filled with stakes. He mocked us for a while, then agreed to trade Shancus's life for Darius's. But he lied. Instead of releasing the snake-boy, he killed him brutally. I still had hold of Darius. In a blind, cold rage, I prepared to murder him for revenge. But just before I stabbed the boy, Steve stopped me with his cruelest revelation yet — Darius's mother was my sister, Annie. If I murdered Steve's son, I'd be killing my own nephew.

And with that he departed, cackling like the demon he was, leaving me to the madness of the blood-drenched night.

PART ONE

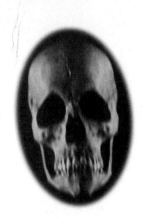

CHAPTER ONE

SITTING ON THE STAGE. Gazing around the theater. Remembering the thrilling show I saw the first time I came. Comparing it to tonight's warped "entertainment." Feeling very small and lonely.

Vancha didn't lose his head, even when Steve played his trump card. He kept going, picked his way through the pit of stakes to the stage, then raced down the tunnel that Steve, Gannen, and R.V. had fled through. It led to the streets at the rear of the theater. No way of telling which way they'd gone. He returned, cursing with fury. When he saw Shancus, lying dead on the stage like a bird with a broken neck, he stopped and sank to his knees.

Evra was next across, following Vancha's route through the stakes, crying out Shancus's name, screaming for him not to die, even though he must have known it was too late, that his son was already dead. We should have held him back — he fell and pierced himself several times, and could easily have perished — but we were frozen with shock and horror.

Fortunately Evra made it to the stage without injuring himself too severely. Once there, he slumped beside Shancus, desperately checked for signs of life, then howled with loss. Sobbing and moaning with grief, he cradled the dead boy's head in his lap, tears dripping onto his son's motionless face. The rest of us watched from a distance. We were all crying bitterly, even the normally steel-faced Alice Burgess.

In time, Harkat also climbed through the stakes. There was a long plank on the stage. He and Vancha extended it over the pit so that the rest of us could join them. I don't think anybody really wanted to go up there. For a long moment none of us moved. Then Debbie, sobbing with deep, wracking gulps, stumbled to the plank and hauled herself up.

Alice crossed the pit next. I brought up the rear. I was shaking uncontrollably. I wanted to turn and run. Earlier, I thought I knew how I'd feel if our gamble backfired and Steve killed Shancus. But I'd known nothing. I never truly expected Steve to murder the snake-boy. I'd let R.V. march the boy into Steve's den, certain no harm would come to my honorary godson.

CHAPTER ONE

Now that Steve had made a fool of me (yet again) and slaughtered Shancus, all I wanted was to be dead. I couldn't feel pain if I was dead. No shame. No guilt. I wouldn't have to look Evra in the eye, knowing I was responsible for his son's needless, shocking death.

We'd forgotten about Darius. I hadn't killed him — how could I kill my own nephew? Following Steve's triumphant revelation, the hatred and anger that had filled me like a fire drained away from me in an instant. I released Darius, having lost my murderous interest in him, and just left him on the far side of the pit.

Evanna was standing near the boy, idly picking at one of the ropes that encircled her body — she preferred ropes to ordinary clothes. It was clear from the witch's stance that she wouldn't interfere if Darius made a break for freedom. It would have been the simplest thing in the world for him to escape. But he didn't. He stood, sentry-like, trembling, waiting for us to summon him.

Finally Alice stumbled over to me, wiping tears from her face. "We should take them back to the Cirque Du Freak," she said, nodding at Evra and Shancus.

"In a while," I agreed, dreading the moment I'd have to face Evra. And what about Merla, Shancus's mother? Would *I* have to break the terrible news to her?

"No — now," Alice said firmly. "Harkat and Debbie

can take them. We need to straighten some things out before we leave." She nodded at Darius, tiny and vulnerable under the glare of the lights.

"I don't want to talk about this," I groaned.

"I know," she said. "But we must. The boy might know where Steve is staying. If he does, this is the time to strike. They won't expect —"

"How can you even think about such things?" I hissed angrily. "Shancus is dead! Don't you care?"

She slapped my face. I blinked, stunned. "You're not a child, Darren, so don't act like one," she said coldly. "Of course I care. But we can't bring him back, and we'll achieve nothing by standing around, moping. We need to act. Only in swift revenge can we maybe find a small sliver of comfort."

She was right. Self-pity was a waste. Revenge was essential. As hard as it was, I dug myself out of my misery and set about sending Shancus's body home. Harkat didn't want to leave Evra and Debbie. He wanted to stay and chase Steve with us. But somebody had to help carry Shancus. He accepted his task reluctantly, but made me promise we wouldn't face Steve without him. "I've come too far with you to . . . miss out now. I want to be there when you . . . cut the demon down."

Debbie threw her arms around me before leaving. "How could he do it?" she cried. "Even a monster couldn't . . . wouldn't . . ."

"Steve's more than a monster," I replied numbly. I wanted to return her embrace, but my arms wouldn't work. Alice pried her away from me. She gave Debbie a handkerchief and whispered something to her. Debbie sniffed miserably, nodded, gave Alice a hug, then went to stand beside Evra.

I wanted to talk with Evra before he left, but I could think of nothing to say. If he'd confronted me, maybe I'd have responded, but he had eyes only for his lifeless son. Dead people often look like they're sleeping. Shancus didn't. He'd been a vibrant, buzzing, active child. All that vitality was lost now. Nobody could have looked upon him and thought he was anything but dead.

I remained standing until Evra, Debbie, and Harkat had departed, Harkat carrying Shancus's body tenderly in his thick, grey arms. Then I slid to the floor and sat there for ages, staring around in a daze, thinking about the past and my first visit here, using the theater and my memories as a barrier between me and my grief.

Eventually Vancha and Alice approached. I don't know how long the pair had been talking together, but when they came to stand before me they'd wiped their faces clean of tears and looked ready for business.

"Will I talk to the boy or do you want to?" Vancha asked gruffly.

"I don't care," I sighed. Then, glancing at Darius, who still stood alone with Evanna in the vastness of the auditorium, I said, "I'll do it."

"Darius," Alice called. His head rose immediately. "Come here."

Darius went straight to the plank, climbed up, and walked across. He had an excellent sense of balance. I found myself thinking that was probably a by-product of his vampaneze blood — Steve had pumped some of his own blood into his son, turning him into a half-vampaneze. Thinking that, I began to hate the boy again. My fingers twitched in anticipation of grabbing him by the throat and . . .

But then I recalled his face when he'd learned he was my nephew — shock, terror, confusion, pain, remorse — and my hatred for the boy died away.

Darius walked directly up to us. If he was afraid — and he must have been — he masked it bravely. Stopping, he stared at Vancha, then at Alice, finally at me. Now that I studied him closely, I saw a certain family resemblance. Thinking about that, I frowned.

"You're not the boy I saw before," I said. Darius looked at me uncertainly. "I went to my old home when we first came to town," I explained. "I watched from behind the fence. I saw Annie. She was bringing in laundry. Then you arrived and came out to help her. Except it wasn't *you*. It was a chubby boy with fair hair."

"Oggy Bas," Darius said after a second's thought. "My friend. I remember that day. He came home with me. I sent him out to help Mom while I was taking my shoes off. Oggy always does what I tell him." Then, licking his lips nervously, he looked around at all of us again and said, "I didn't know." It wasn't an apology, just a statement of fact. "Dad told me vampires were evil. He said you were the worst of the lot. 'Darren the cruel, Darren the mad, Darren the baby-killer.' But he never mentioned your last name."

Evanna had crossed the plank after Darius and was circling us, studying us as if we were chess pieces. I ignored her — there'd be time for the witch later.

"What did Steve tell you about the vampaneze?" I asked Darius.

"That they wanted to stop vampires killing humans. They broke away from the clan several hundred years ago and had battled to stop the slaughter of humans ever since. They drank only small amounts of blood when they fed, just enough to survive."

"You believed him?" Vancha snorted.

"He was my dad," Darius answered. "He was always kind to me. I never saw him like I saw him tonight. I had no reason to doubt him."

"But you doubt him now," Alice noted wryly.

"Yes. He's evil." As soon as he said it, Darius burst into tears, his brave front collapsing. It couldn't have been easy for a child to admit his father was evil. Even in the midst of my grief and fury, I felt pity for the boy.

"What about Annie?" I asked when Darius had recovered enough to speak again. "Did Steve feed her the same sort of lies?"

"She doesn't know," Darius said. "They haven't spoken since before I was born. I never told her I was meeting him."

I breathed a small sigh of relief. I'd had a sudden, terrifying flash of Annie as Steve's consort, having grown up as bitter and twisted as him. It was good to know she wasn't part of this dark insanity.

"Do you want to tell him the truth about vampires and vampaneze, or will I?" Vancha asked.

"First things first," Alice interrupted. "Does he know where his father is?"

"No," Darius said sadly. "I always met him here. This is where he was based. If he has another hideout, I don't know about it."

"Damn!" Alice snarled.

"No ideas at all?" I asked. Darius thought for a moment, then shook his head. I glanced at Vancha. "Will you set him straight?"

"Sure." Vancha quickly filled Darius in on the truth. He told him that the vampaneze were the ones who killed when they drank, though he was careful to describe their ways in detail — they kept part of a person's spirit alive within themselves when they drained a human dry, so they didn't look upon it as murder. They were noble. They never lied. They weren't deliberately evil.

"Then your father came along," Vancha said, and explained about the Lord of the Vampaneze, the War of the Scars, Mr. Tiny's prediction, and our part in it.

"I don't understand," Darius said at the end, forehead creased. "If the vampaneze don't lie, how come Dad lied all the time? And he taught me how to use an arrow-gun, but you said they can't use such weapons."

"They're not supposed to," Vancha said. "I haven't seen or heard of any others breaking those rules. But their Lord's above such laws. They worship him so much — or fear what will happen if they disobey him — that they don't care what he does, as long as he leads them to victory over the vampires."

Darius thought about that in silence for a long time. He was only ten years old, but he had the expression and manner of someone much older.

"I wouldn't have helped if I'd known," he said in the end. "I grew up thinking vampires were evil, like in the movies. When Dad came to me a few years ago and said he was on a mission to stop them, I thought it was a great adventure. I thought he was a hero. I was proud to be his son. I'd have done anything for him. I *did* . . ."

He looked like he was about to cry again. But then his jaw firmed and he stared at me. "But how did *you* get involved in this?" he asked. "Mom told me you died. She said you broke your neck."

"I faked my death," I said, and gave him a very brief rundown of my early life as a vampire's assistant, sacrificing everything I held dear to save Steve's life.

"But why does he hate you if you saved him?" Darius shouted. "That's crazy!"

"Steve sees things differently," I shrugged. "He believes it was his destiny to become a vampire. He thinks I stole his rightful place. He's determined to make me pay."

Darius shook his head, confused. "I can't understand that," he said.

"You're young," I smiled sadly. "You have a lot to learn about people and how they operate." I fell silent, thinking that those were some of the many things poor Shancus would never learn.

"So," Darius said a while later, breaking the silence. "What happens now?"

"Go home," I sighed. "Forget about this. Put it behind you."

"But what about the vampaneze?" Darius cried. "Dad's still out there. I want to help you find him."

"Really?" I looked at him icily. "You want to help us kill him? You'd lead us to your own father and watch while we cut his rotten heart out?"

Darius shifted uneasily. "He's evil," he whispered.

"Yes," I agreed. "But he's still your father. You're better off out of this."

"And Mom?" Darius asked. "What do I tell her?"

"Nothing," I said. "She thinks I'm dead. Let her go on thinking that. Say nothing of this. The world I live in isn't a fit world for children — and as a child who's lived in it, I should know! Take back your ordinary life. Try not to dwell on what's happened. In time you might be able to dismiss all this as a horrible dream." I placed my hands on his shoulders and smiled warmly. "Go home, Darius. Be good to Annie. Make her happy."

Darius wasn't pleased, but I could see him making up his mind to accept my advice. Then Vancha spoke. "It's not that easy."

"What?" I frowned.

"He's in. He can't opt out."

"Of course he can!" I snapped.

Vancha shook his head stubbornly. "He was blooded. The vampaneze blood is thin in him, but it will thicken. He won't age like normal children, and in a few decades the purge will strike and he'll become a full-vampaneze." Vancha sighed. "But his real problems will start long before then."

"What do you mean?" I croaked, though I sensed what he was getting at.

"*Feeding,*" Vancha said. He turned his gaze on Darius. "You'll need to drink blood to survive."

Darius stiffened, then grinned shakily. "So I'll drink like you guys," he said. "A drop here, a drop there. I don't mind. It'll be kind of cool, in a way. Maybe I'll drink from my teachers and —"

"No," Vancha growled. "You can't drink like us. In the beginning, vampaneze were the same as vampires, except in their customs. But they've changed. The centuries have altered them physically. Now a vampaneze *must* kill when he feeds. They're driven to it. They have no choice or control. I was once a half-vampaneze, so I know what I'm speaking about."

Vancha drew himself up straight and spoke sadly but firmly. "In a few months the hunger will grow within you. You won't be able to resist. You'll drink blood because you have to, and when you drink, because you're a half-vampaneze — you'll *kill!*"

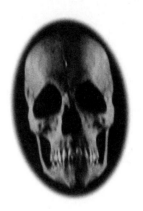

CHAPTER TWO

WE MARCHED IN SILENCE, in single file, Darius leading the way like Oliver Twist at the head of a funeral procession. Following the massacre at the stadium after the soccer match, a series of roadblocks had been set in place around the town. But there weren't many in this area, so we made good time, having to take only a couple of short detours. I was at the back of the line, a few yards behind the others, worrying about the meeting to come. I'd agreed to it easily enough in the theater, but now that we were getting closer, I was having second thoughts.

While I was running through my words, thinking of all the things I could and should say, Evanna slipped back to walk along beside me. "If it helps, the snake-boy's soul has flown straight to Paradise," she said.

"I never thought otherwise," I replied stiffly, glaring at her hatefully.

"Why such a dark look?" she asked, genuine surprise in her mismatched green and brown eyes.

"You knew it was coming," I growled. "You could have warned us and saved Shancus."

"No," she snapped, irritated. "Why do you people level the same accusations at me over and over? You know I have the power to see into the future, but not the power to directly influence it. I cannot act to change that which is to be. Nor could my brother."

"Why not?" I snarled. "You always say that terrible things will happen if you do, but what are they? What could be worse than letting an innocent child die at the hands of a monster?"

Evanna was quiet a moment, then spoke softly, so that only I could hear. "There are worse monsters than Steve Leonard, and worse even than the Lord of the Shadows — be he Steve or you. These other monsters wait in the timeless wings around the stage of the world, never seen by man, but always seeing, always hungering, always eager to break through.

"I am bound by laws older than mankind. So was my brother and so, to a large extent, is my father. If I took advantage of the present, and tried to change the course of a future I knew about, I'd break the laws of the universe. The monsters I speak of would then be free to cross into this world, and it would become a cauldron of endless, bloody savagery."

"It seems that way already," I said sourly.

"For you, perhaps," she agreed. "But for billions of others it is not. Would you have everyone suffer as you have — and worse?"

"Of course not," I muttered. "But you told me they were going to suffer anyway, that the Lord of the Shadows will destroy mankind."

"He will bring it to its knees," she said. "But he will not crush it entirely. Hope will remain. One day, far in the future, humans might rise again. If I interfered and unleashed the real monsters, hope would become a word without meaning."

I didn't know what to think about these other monsters of Evanna's — it was the first time she'd ever spoken of such creatures — so I brought the conversation back to center on the monster I knew all too much about. "You're wrong when you say I can become the Lord of the Shadows," I said, trying to change my destiny by denying it. "I'm not a monster."

"You would have killed Darius if Steve hadn't said he was your nephew," Evanna reminded me.

I recalled the hateful fury that had flared to life inside me when I saw Shancus die. In that moment I became like Steve. I didn't care about right or wrong. I only wanted to hurt my enemy by killing his son. I'd seen a glimpse of my future then, the beast I could become, but I didn't want to believe it was real.

"That would have been in revenge for Shancus," I said bitterly, trying to hide from the truth. "It wouldn't have been the act of an out-of-control beast. I wouldn't become a monster just because of a single execution."

"No?" Evanna challenged me. "There was a time when you thought differently. Do you remember when you killed your first vampaneze, in the caves of Vampire Mountain? You wept afterwards. You thought killing was wrong. You believed there were ways to resolve differences other than through violence."

"I still do," I said, but my words sounded hollow, even to me.

"You would not have tried to take the life of a child if you did," Evanna said, stroking the hairs of her beard. "You have changed, Darren. You're not evil like Steve, but you carry the seeds of evil within you. Your intentions are good, but time and circumstance will see you become that which you despise. This world will warp you and, despite your noble wishes, the monster within you will grow. Friends will become enemies. Truths will become lies. Beliefs will become sick jokes.

"The path of revenge is always lined with danger. By following the ways of those you hate, you risk turning into them. This is your destiny, Darren Shan. You cannot avoid it. Unless Steve kills you and he becomes the Lord of the Shadows instead."

"What about Vancha?" I hissed. "What if he kills Steve? Can't *he* become your bloody Lord of the Shadows?"

"No," she said calmly. "Vancha has the power to kill Steve and decide the fate of the War of the Scars. But moving beyond that, it's either you or Steve. There is no other. Death or monstrosity. Those are your options."

She moved ahead of me then, leaving me with my troubled, frantic thoughts. Was there truly no hope for me or the world? And if not, if I was trapped between death at the hands of Steve or replacing him as the Lord of the Shadows, which was preferable? Was it better to live and terrorize the world — or die now, while I was still halfway human?

I couldn't decide on an answer. There didn't seem to be one. And so I trudged along miserably and let my thoughts return to the more pressing issue — what to say to my grown-up sister who'd buried me as a child.

———

Twenty minutes later, Darius opened the back door and held it ajar. I paused, staring at the house, filled with a sense of foreboding. Vancha and Alice were behind me, and Evanna farther behind them. I looked back at my friends pleadingly. "Do I really have to do this?" I croaked.

"Yes," Vancha said. "It would be wrong to risk his life without informing his mother first. She must decide."

"OK," I sighed. "You'll wait out here till I call?"

"Aye."

I gulped, then stepped over the threshold into the house where I'd lived as a boy. After eighteen long years of wandering, I had finally come home.

Darius guided me to the living room, though I could have found my way blindfolded. Much had changed within the house — new wallpaper and carpets, furniture, and light fittings — but it felt the same, warm and comfy, layered with memories of the distant past. It was like walking through a ghost house — except the house was real and I was the ghost.

Darius pushed the living-room door open. And there was Annie, her brown hair tied up in a bun, sitting in a chair in front of the TV, sipping hot chocolate, watching the news. "Decided to come home at last, did you?" she said to Darius, catching sight of him out of the corner of her eye. She laid the cup of hot chocolate down. "I was worried. Have you seen the news? There's —"

She saw me entering the room after Darius. "Is this one of your friends?" she asked. I could see her thinking I looked too old to be his friend. She was instantly suspicious of me.

"Hello, Annie," I said, smiling nervously, advancing into the light.

"Have we met before?" she asked, frowning, not recognizing me.

"In a way," I chuckled drily.

"Mom, it's —" Darius started to say.

"No," I interrupted. "Let her see for herself. Don't tell her."

"Tell me what?" Annie snapped. She was squinting at me now, uneasy.

"Look closer, Annie," I said softly, walking across the room, stopping just a few feet away from her. "Look at my eyes. They say the eyes never really change, even if everything else does."

"Your voice," she muttered. "There's something about . . ." She stood — she was the same height as me — and gazed steadily into my eyes. I smiled.

"You look like somebody I knew a long time ago," Annie said. "But I don't remember who . . ."

"You did know me a long time ago," I whispered. "Eighteen years ago."

"Nonsense!" Annie snorted. "You'd have only been a baby."

"No," I said. "I've aged slowly. I was slightly older than Darius when you last saw me."

"Is this a joke?" she half laughed.

"Look at him, Mom," Darius said intently. "Really *look* at him."

And she did. And this time I saw something in her expression and realized she'd known who I was the second she saw me — she just hadn't admitted it to herself yet.

"Listen to your instincts, Annie," I said. "You always had good instincts. If I'd had your nose for trouble, maybe I wouldn't have gotten into this mess. Maybe I'd have had more sense than to steal a poisonous spider . . ."

Annie's eyes widened. "No!" she gasped.

"Yes," I said.

"You can't be!"

"I am."

"But . . . *No!*" she growled, firmly this time. "I don't know who put you up to this, or what you think you'll achieve by it, but if you don't get out quick, I'll —"

"I bet you never told anyone about Madam Octa,"

I cut her off. She trembled at the mention of the spider's name. "I bet you kept that secret all these years. You must have guessed she had something to do with my 'death.' Maybe you asked Steve about it, since he was the one she bit, but I bet you never told Mom or —"

"Darren?" she wheezed, confused tears springing to her eyes.

"Hi, sis," I grinned. "Long time no see."

She starred at me, appalled, and then did something I thought only happened in corny old movies — her eyes rolled up, her legs gave way, and she fainted!

Annie sat in her chair, a fresh mug of hot chocolate cupped between her hands. I sat opposite her in a chair I'd dragged over from the other side of the room. Darius stood by the TV, which he'd turned off shortly after Annie fainted. Annie hadn't said much since recovering. Once she'd come to, she'd pressed back into her chair, gazed at me, torn between horror and hope, and simply gasped, *"How?"*

I'd spent the time since then filling her in. I spoke quietly and rapidly, starting with Mr. Crepsley and Madam Octa, explaining the deal I'd struck to save Steve's life, giving her a quick rundown of the years since then; my existence as a vampire, the vampaneze, the War of the Scars, tracking the Vampaneze Lord. I didn't tell her Steve was the Lord or involved with the vampaneze — I wanted to see how she reacted to the rest of the story before hitting her with that one.

Her eyes didn't betray her feelings. It was impossible to guess what she was thinking. When I got to the part of the story involving Darius, her gaze slid from me to her son, and she leaned forward slightly as I described how he'd been tricked into aiding the vampaneze, again being careful not to refer to Steve by name. I finished with my return to the old movie theater, Shancus's death, and the Vampaneze Lord's revelation that Darius was my nephew.

"Once Darius knew the truth, he was horrified," I said. "But I told him he mustn't blame himself. Lots of older and wiser people than him have been fooled by the Lord of the Vampaneze."

I stopped and waited for her reaction. It wasn't long coming.

"You're insane," she said coldly. "If you *are* my brother — and I'm not a hundred percent convinced — then whatever disease stunted your growth also affected your brain. Vampires? Vampaneze? My son in league with a killer?" she sneered. "You're a madman."

"But it's true!" Darius exclaimed. "He can prove it! He's stronger and faster than any human. He can —"

"Be quiet!" Annie roared with such venom that Darius shut up instantly. She glared at me furiously. "Get out of my house," she snarled. "Stay away from my son. Don't ever come back."

"But —" I began.

"No!" she screamed. "You're not my brother! Even if you are, you're not! We buried Darren eighteen years ago. He's dead and that's the way I want him to stay. I don't care if you're him or not. I want you out of my life — *our* lives — immediately." She stood and pointed at the door. *"Go!"*

I didn't move. I wanted to. If it hadn't been for Darius, I would have slunk out like a kicked dog. But she had to know what her son had become. I couldn't leave without convincing her of the danger he was in.

While Annie stood, pointing at the door, hand trembling wildly, face twisted with rage, Darius stepped away from the TV. "Mom," he said quietly. "Don't you want to know how I fell in with the vampaneze and why I helped them?"

"There are no vampaneze!" she yelled. "This maniac has filled your imagination with lies and —"

"Steve Leonard's the Lord of the Vampaneze," Darius

said, and Annie stopped dead. "He came to me a few years ago," Darius went on, edging slowly toward her. "At first we just went for walks together, he took me to the movies and took me out to eat, stuff like that. He told me not to say anything to you. He said you wouldn't like it, that you'd make him go away."

He stopped in front of her, reached up, took hold of her pointing hand, and gently bent her arms down. She was staring at him wordlessly. "He's my dad," Darius said sadly. "I trusted him because I thought he loved me. That's why I believed him when he told me about vampires. He said he was telling me for my protection, that he was worried about me — and *you*. He wanted to protect us. That's where it began. Then I got more involved. He taught me how to use a knife, how to shoot, how to kill."

Annie sank back into her chair, unable to respond.

"It was Steve," Darius said. "Steve who got me into trouble, who killed the snake-boy, who made Darren come back to see you. Darren didn't want to — he knew he'd hurt you — but Steve left him with no choice. It's true, Mom, everything he said. You've got to believe us, because it was Steve, and I think he might come back — come after *you* — and if we aren't ready ... if you don't believe ..."

He ground to a halt, running out of words. But

he'd said enough. When Annie looked at me again, there was fear and doubt in her eyes, but no scorn. *"Steve?"* she moaned. I nodded unhappily and her face hardened. "What did I tell you about him?" she screamed at Darius, grabbing the boy and shaking him angrily. "I told you never to go near him! That if you ever saw him, you had to run and tell me! I said he was dangerous!"

"I didn't believe you!" Darius cried. "I thought you hated him just because he ran away, that you were lying! He was my dad!" He tore himself away from her and collapsed on the floor, weeping. "He was my dad," he sobbed again. "I loved him."

Annie stared at Darius crying. Then she stared at me. And then she also started to cry, and her sobs were even deeper and more painful than her son's.

I didn't cry. I was saving my tears. I knew the worst was yet to come.

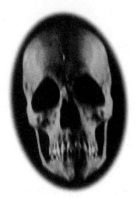

CHAPTER THREE

LATER. AFTER THE TEARS. Sitting around the living room. Annie had recovered from the worst of the shock. All three of us were drinking hot chocolate. I hadn't called the others in yet — I wanted some personal time with Annie before I dumped the full fallout from the War of the Scars upon her.

Annie made me tell her more about my life. She wanted to hear about the countries I'd visited, the people I'd met, the adventures I'd had. I told her some of the highlights, leaving out the darker aspects. She listened, dazed, touching me every few minutes to make sure I was real. When she heard I was a Prince, she laughed with delight. "Does that make me a princess?" she smiled.

"Afraid not," I chuckled.

In return, Annie told me what her life had been like.

The hard months after I'd "died." Slowly returning to normal. She was young, so she recovered, but Mom and Dad never really got over it. She raised the question of whether or not they should be told I was alive. Then, before I could speak, she said, "No. They're happy now. It's too late to change the past. Best not to drag it up again."

I paid close attention when she spoke about Steve. "I was a teenager," she said angrily, "mixed-up and unsure of myself. I had some friends but not many. And no serious boyfriend. Then Steve came back. He was only a few years older than me, but he looked and acted grown-up. And he was interested in me. He wanted to talk to me. He treated me like an equal."

They spent a lot of time together. Steve put on a good act — kind, generous, loving. Annie thought he cared for her, that they had a future together. She fell in love with him, and gave her love to him. Then she found out she was expecting a baby.

"His face lit up when he heard," she said, shivering from the memory. Darius was by her side, solemn, silent, listening intently. "He made me believe he was delighted, that we'd get married and have lots of children together. He told me not to tell anyone — he wanted to keep it secret until we were husband and wife. He went away again. He said it was to earn money, to pay for our wedding and the baby's upkeep. He stayed away a long time. He returned late one night, while I was sleeping. Woke me up. Before I could say anything, he clamped a hand over my mouth and laughed. 'Too late to stop it now!' he mocked me. He said other things, horrible things. Then he left. I haven't heard from him since."

She had to tell Mom and Dad about the baby then. They were furious — not with her, but with Steve. Dad would have killed Steve if he'd found him. But nobody knew where Steve was. He'd vanished.

"Raising Darius was hard," she said and smiled, ruffling his hair, "but I wouldn't give up a day of it. Steve was wicked, but he gave me the most marvelous gift anyone could have ever given me."

"Soppy old cow," Darius grunted, fighting hard not to smile.

I was quiet a long time after that. I wondered if Steve had meant to use Darius against me even then. This was back before he met the vampaneze and learned of his abominable destiny. But I bet he was already planning my downfall, one way or the other. Did he deliberately get Annie pregnant, so he could use his nephew or niece to hurt me? Knowing Steve as I did, I guessed those were his exact intentions.

Annie started telling me about her life with Darius,

how Mom and Dad helped rear him until they moved away, and how the pair were managing now on their own. She worried about him not having a father, but her experience with Steve had made her wary of men, and she found it hard to trust anyone. I could have listened to Annie talk all night, telling tales about Mom, Dad, and Darius. I was catching up on all those missed years. I felt like part of the family again. I didn't want to stop.

But we were in the middle of a crisis. I'd delayed the moment of truth, but now I had to tell her about it. The night was coming on, and I was eager to conclude the business I'd come about. I let her finish the story she was telling — about Darius's first week in school — then asked if I could introduce her to some of my friends.

Annie wasn't sure what to make of Vancha, Alice, and Evanna. Alice dressed normally, but Vancha in his animal hides, with his straps of throwing stars and green hair, and the hirsute, deliriously ugly Evanna draped in robes . . . They would have stuck out like a couple of gargoyles anywhere!

But they were my friends (well, Vancha and Alice were; I wasn't sure about the witch), so Annie welcomed them — though I could tell she didn't entirely trust the trio. And I knew she sensed they weren't here just to make up the numbers. She guessed that something bad was coming.

We made small talk for a while. Alice told Annie about her years on the police force, Vancha described some of his Princely duties, and Evanna gave her tips on how to breed frogs (not that Annie had any interest in that!). Then Darius yawned. Vancha looked at me meaningfully — it was time.

"Annie," I started hesitantly, "I told you Darius pledged himself to the vampaneze. But I didn't tell you what exactly that means."

"Go on," Annie said when I stalled.

"Steve blooded him," I said. "He transferred some of his vampaneze blood to Darius. The blood isn't very strong within him, but it will strengthen. The cells will multiply and take over."

"You're saying he'll become like you?" Annie's face was ashen. "He won't age normally? He'll need to drink blood to survive?"

"Yes." Her face crumpled — she thought that was the worst, the part I'd been holding back. I wished I could spare her the truth, but I couldn't. "There's more," I said, and she stiffened. "Vampires can control their feeding habits. It isn't easy — it requires training — but we can. Vampaneze can't. Their blood forces them to kill every time they feed."

"No!" Annie moaned. "Darius isn't a killer! He wouldn't!"

"He would," Vancha grunted. "He'd have no choice. Once a vampaneze gets the taste of blood, his urges consume him. He goes into a kind of trance and feeds until he's drained the source dry. He can't stop."

"But there must be some way to help him!" Annie insisted. "Doctors . . . surgery . . . medicine . . ."

"No," Vancha said. "This isn't a human disease. Your doctors could study him, and restrain him while he was feeding — but do you want your son to spend his life imprisoned?"

"Also," I said, "they couldn't stop him when he was older. As he comes into his full powers, he'll grow incredibly strong. They'd have to keep him comatose to control him."

"No!" Annie shouted, her face dark with stubborn rage. "I won't allow this! There must be a way to save him!"

"There is," I said, and she relaxed slightly. "But it's dangerous. And it won't restore his humanity — it will merely drive him toward a different corner of the night."

"Don't talk in riddles!" Annie snapped. "What does he have to do?"

"Become a vampire," I said.

Annie stared at me in disbelief.

"It's not as bad as it sounds," I went on quickly. "Yes, he'd age slowly, but that's something you and he could learn to cope with. And yes, he'd have to drink blood, but he wouldn't harm when he drank. We'd teach him to master his urges."

"No," Annie said. "There must be another way."

"There isn't," Vancha huffed. "And even this way isn't certain. Nor is it safe."

"I'll have to trade blood with him," I explained. "Pump my vampire cells into his body and accept his vampaneze cells into mine. The vampire and vampaneze cells will attack each other. If all goes well, Darius will become a half-vampire and I'll carry on as before."

"But if it fails, you'll become a half-vampaneze and Darius won't change?" Annie guessed, trembling at the thought of such a horrible fate.

"No," I said. "It's worse than that. If it fails, I'll die — and so will Darius."

And then I sat back numbly and awaited her decision.

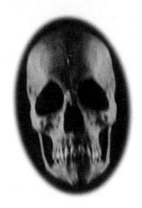

CHAPTER FOUR

ANNIE DIDN'T LIKE IT — nobody did! — but we eventually convinced her that there was no other solution. She wanted to wait, think it over, and discuss it with her doctor, but I told her it was now or never. "Vancha and I have a mission to complete," I reminded her. "We might not be able to come back later."

When we'd first discussed the transfusion, Vancha had volunteered. He didn't think it was safe for me to try. I was in the middle of the purge — my vampire cells were taking over, turning me into a full-vampire, and my body was in a state of flux. But when I pressed him, he admitted there was no real reason for thinking that the purge would have any effect on the procedure. It might even work in our favor — since my vampire cells were hyperactive, they might stand a better chance of destroying the vampaneze cells.

We'd tried to quiz Evanna about the dangers. She could look into the future and tell us whether it would succeed or not. But she refused to be drawn. "This has nothing to do with me," she'd said. "I will not comment on it."

"But it must be safe," I'd pressed, hoping for reassurance. "We're destined to meet Steve again. We can't do that if I die."

"Your final encounter with Steve Leonard is by no means set in stone," she'd replied. "If you die beforehand, he will become the Lord of the Shadows by default and the war will swing the way of the vampaneze. Do not think you are immune to danger because of your destiny, Darren — you *can* and perhaps *will* die if you attempt this."

But Darius was my nephew. Vancha didn't approve — he would have preferred to overlook Darius for the time being, and focus on Steve — but I couldn't leave the boy this way, with such a threat hanging over him. If I could save him, I must.

We could have handled the blood transfer with syringes, but Darius insisted on the traditional fingertips method. He was excited, despite the danger, and wanted to do it the old way. "If I'm going to be a vampire, I want to be a real one," he growled. "I don't want to hide my marks. It's all or nothing."

"But it'll be painful," I warned him.

"I don't care," he sniffed.

Annie's doubts remained, but in the end she agreed to the plan. She might not have if Darius had wavered, but he stuck to his guns with grim determination. I hated to admit it — and I didn't say it out loud — but he had his father's sense of commitment. Steve was insanely evil, but he always did what he set out to do, and nothing could change his mind once he'd made it up. Darius was the same.

"I can't believe this is happening," Annie sighed as I sat opposite Darius and prepared to drive my nails into the tips of his fingers. "Earlier tonight I was only thinking about doing the shopping tomorrow, and being here to let Darius in when he got home from school. Then my brother walks back into my life and tells me he's a vampire! And now, as I'm just getting used to that, I might lose him as swiftly as I found him — and my son too!"

She almost called it off then, but Alice stepped up behind her and said softly, "Would you rather lose him when he's human, or when he's a killer like his father?" It was a cruel thing to say, but it steadied Annie's nerves and reminded her of what was at stake. Trembling fiercely, weeping quietly, she stepped away and let me proceed.

Without any warning, I dug my nails into the soft flesh at the tips of Darius's fingers. He yelped painfully and jerked back in his chair. "Don't," I said as he raised his fingers to his mouth to suck them. "Let them bleed."

Darius lowered his hands. Gritting my teeth, I dug my right-hand nails into my left-hand fingertips, then did it the other way round. Blood welled up from ten fleshy springs. I pressed my fingers against Darius's and held them there while my blood flowed into his body, and his into mine.

We remained locked for twenty seconds . . . thirty . . . more. I could feel the vampaneze cells as soon as his blood entered my veins, itching, burning, sizzling. I ignored the pain. I could see that Darius was also aware of the change, and that it was hurting him more than me. I pressed closer against him, so it was impossible for him to break away.

Vancha stood guard, observing us, calculating. When he thought the time was right, he grabbed my arms and pulled my hands away. I gasped out loud, stood, half smiled, then fell to the floor, writhing in agony. I hadn't expected the cells to kick in so soon, and was unprepared for the brutal speed of the reaction.

During my convulsions, I saw Darius twisting sharply in his chair, eyes bulging, making choking noises, arms and legs thrashing wildly. Annie hurried

toward him, but Vancha knocked her aside. "Don't interfere!" he barked. "Nature must take its course. We
can't get in its way."

For several minutes I jackknifed wildly on the floor.
It felt like I was on fire inside my skin. I'd experienced
blinding headaches and loads of discomfort during the
purge, but this took me to new heights of pain. Pressure built at the back of my eyes, as though my brain
was going to bulge out through my eye sockets. I dug
the heels of my hands hard into my eyes, then into the
sides of my head. I don't know if I was roaring or
wheezing — I could hear nothing.

I vomited, then dry-heaved. I crashed into something hard — the TV. I rolled away from it and smashed
into a wall. I dug my nails into the plaster and brick, trying to make the pain go away.

Finally the pressure subsided. My limbs relaxed. I
stopped dry-heaving. Sight and sound returned, though
my fierce headache remained. I looked around, dazed.
Vancha was crouching over me, wiping my face clean,
smiling. "You've come through it," he said. "You'll be
OK — with the luck of the vampires."

"Darius?" I gasped.

Vancha raised my head and pointed. Darius was lying on the couch, eyes closed, perfectly still, Annie and
Alice kneeling beside him. Evanna sat in a corner, head

bowed. For a horrifying moment I thought Darius was dead. Then I saw his chest lift softly and fall, and I knew he was just asleep.

"He'll be fine," Vancha said. "We'll have to keep a close eye on the two of you for a few nights. You'll probably have further fits, less severe than this one. But most who attempt this die of the first seizure. Having survived that, the odds are good for both of you."

I sat up wearily. Vancha took my fingers and spat on them, rubbing his spit in to help close the wounds.

"I feel awful," I moaned.

"You won't improve anytime soon," Vancha said. "When I turned from vampanizm to vampirism it took my system a month to settle down, and almost a year to get back to normal. And you've got the purge to contend with too." He chuckled wryly. "You're in for some rough nights, Sire!"

Vancha helped me back to my chair. Alice asked if I'd like water or milk to drink. Vancha said blood would be better for me. Without blinking, Alice used a knife to cut herself and let me feed directly from the wound. Vancha closed the cut with his spit when I was finished. He beamed up at Alice. "You're some woman, Miss Burgess."

"The best," Alice replied drily.

I leaned back, eyes half-closed. "I could sleep for a week," I sighed.

"Why don't you?" Vancha said. "You've only recently recovered from a life-threatening wound. You're in the middle of the purge. You've pulled off the most dangerous blood transfusion known to vampires. By the black blood of Harnon Oan, you've earned a rest!"

"But Steve . . ." I muttered.

"Leonard can wait," Vancha grunted. "We'll send Annie and Darius out of town — Alice will escort them — then get you settled in at the Cirque. A week in your hammock will do you the world of good."

"I guess," I said unhappily. I was thinking about Evra and Merla, and what I could find to say to them. There was Mr. Tall to consider too — everyone at the Cirque Du Freak had loved him. Like Shancus, he was dead because of his association with me. Would the people there hate me because of that?

"Who do you think will take over for Mr. Tall?" I asked.

"I have no idea," Vancha said. "I don't think anybody ever expected him to die, certainly not in such sudden circumstances."

"Maybe they'll break up," I mused. "Go their own

ways, back to whatever they did before they joined. Some might have left the stadium already. I hope —"

"What was that about a stadium?" Annie interrupted. She was still tending to Darius — he was snoring lightly — but she'd overheard us talking.

"The Cirque Du Freak's camped in the old soccer stadium," I explained. "We're going back there when you leave, but I was saying to Vancha that —"

"The news," Annie interrupted again. "You didn't see tonight's news?"

"No."

"I was watching it when you came in," she said, eyes filling with fresh worry. "I didn't know that's where you were based, so I didn't connect it with you."

"Connect what?" I asked edgily.

"Police have surrounded the stadium," Annie said. "They say the people who killed Tom Jones and the others at the soccer match are there. I should have put it together earlier, when you were telling me about Tommy, but . . ." She shook her head angrily, then continued. "They're not letting anyone in or out. When I was watching the news, they hadn't moved in yet. But they said that when they did, they'd go in with full, lethal force. One of the reporters —" She stopped.

"Go on," I said hoarsely.

"He said he'd never seen so many armed police before. He . . ." She gulped and finished in a whisper. "He said they meant to go in as hard as they could. He said it looked like they planned to kill everyone inside."

CHAPTER FIVE

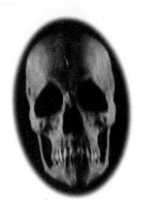

FIRST THINGS FIRST — make sure Annie and Darius got away safely. I couldn't concentrate on helping my friends trapped inside the stadium if I was worrying about my sister and nephew. Once they were free of Steve's influence, safe somewhere he couldn't find them, I could focus on business entirely. Until that time I would only be a distracted liability.

Annie didn't want to go. This was her home and she wanted to fight to protect it. When, after telling her about some of the atrocities Steve had committed over the years, I convinced her they had to leave, she insisted I go with them. For years she'd believed I was dead. Now that she knew otherwise, she didn't want to lose me again so quickly.

"I can't come," I sighed. "Not while my friends are in danger. Later, when it's over, I'll find you."

"Not if Steve kills you!" Annie cried. I had no answer for that one. "What about Darius?" she pressed. "You said he needs training. What will he do without you?"

"Give us your cell phone number," I said. "Alice will contact her people before we go to the stadium. In the worst-case scenario, somebody will get in touch. A vampire will link up with you and instruct Darius, or guide him to Vampire Mountain, where Seba or Vanez can look after him."

"Who?" she asked.

"Old friends," I smiled. "They can teach him everything he'll ever need to know about being a vampire."

Annie kept trying to change my mind, telling me my place was with her and Darius, that I was her brother before I became a vampire and I should think of her first. But she was wrong. I left the human world behind when I became a Vampire Prince. I still cared for Annie and loved her, but my first loyalty was to the clan.

When she realized she couldn't win me over, Annie bundled Darius into the back of their car — he was still sound asleep — and tearfully went to gather some personal belongings. I told her to take as much as she could, and not to come back. If we defeated Steve, she and Darius could return. If not, somebody would fetch the rest of her stuff. The house would have to be sold, and they'd remain in hiding under the protection of the vampire clan, for as long as the clan was capable of looking after them. (I didn't say "Until the clan falls," but that's what I was thinking.) It wouldn't be an ideal life — but it would be better than winding up in the hands of Steve Leopard.

Annie hugged me with all her strength before getting into the car. "It's not fair," she wept. "There's so much you haven't told me, so much I want to know, so much I want to say."

"Me too," I said, blinking away tears. It was a weird feeling. Everything was happening at ten times the speed it should. It had only been a few hours since we returned to the Cirque Du Freak to chat with Mr. Tall, but it felt like weeks had passed. His death, the chase, Morgan James's beheading, the theater, Shancus being slaughtered by Steve, finding out about Darius, coming to see my sister . . . I wanted to put my foot down on the brake, take time out, make sense of all that was going on. But life makes its own rules and sets its own pace. Sometimes you can rein it in and slow it down — other times you can't.

"You really can't come with us?" Annie tried one last time.

"No," I said. "I want to . . . but no."

"Then I wish you all the luck in the world, Darren,"

she moaned. She kissed me, began to say something else, then broke down in tears. Hurling herself into the car, she checked on Darius, then started the engine and roared away, disappearing into the night, leaving me standing outside my old home — heartbroken.

"Are you all right?" Alice asked, creeping up behind me.

"I will be," I replied, wiping tears from my eyes. "I wish I'd been able to say good-bye to Darius."

"It's not good-bye," Alice said. "Just *au revoir*."

"Hopefully," I sighed, though I didn't really believe it. Win or lose, I had a sick feeling in my stomach that tonight was the last time I'd ever see Annie and Darius. I paused a moment to wish them a silent farewell, then turned around, put them from my thoughts, and let all my emotions and energies center on the problems at hand and the dangers faced by my friends at the Cirque Du Freak.

Inside the house, we discussed our next move. Alice was for getting out of town as quickly as possible, abandoning our friends and allies. "Three of us can't make a difference if there are hordes of police stationed around the stadium," she argued. "Steve Leonard remains the priority. The others will have to fend for themselves."

"But they're our friends," I muttered. "We can't just abandon them."

"We must," she insisted. "It doesn't matter how much it hurts. We can't do anything for them now, not without placing our own lives in jeopardy."

"But Evra . . . Harkat . . . *Debbie.*"

"I know," she said, her eyes sad but hard. "But like I said, it doesn't matter how much it hurts. We have to leave them."

"I don't agree," I said. "I think . . ." I stopped, reluctant to voice my belief.

"Go on," Vancha encouraged me.

"I can't explain it," I said slowly, eyes flicking to Evanna, "but I think Steve's there. At the stadium. Waiting for us. He set the police on us before — when Alice was one of them — and I can't see him pulling the same trick twice. It would be boring the second time around. He craves originality and new thrills. I think the police outside are just for cover."

"He could have set a trap in the movie theatre," Vancha mused, taking up my train of thought. "But that wouldn't have been as elaborate as where we fought him before — in the Cavern of Retribution."

"Exactly," I said. "This is our big showdown. He'll

want to go out on a high, with something outlandish. He's as much of a performer as anyone at the Cirque Du Freak. He loves theatrics. He'd relish the idea of a stadium setting. It would be like the ancient gladiator duels in the Colosseum."

"We're in trouble if you're wrong," Alice said uneasily.

"Nothing new about that," Vancha huffed. He cocked an eyebrow at Evanna. "Care to drop us a hint?"

To our astonishment, the witch nodded soberly. "Darren is right. You either go to the stadium now and face your destiny, or flee and hand victory to the vampaneze."

"I thought you couldn't tell us stuff like that," Vancha said, startled.

"The endgame has commenced," Evanna answered cryptically. "I can speak more openly about certain matters now, without altering the future."

"It'd alter it if we turned tail and ran like hell for the hills," Vancha grunted.

"No," Evanna smiled. "It wouldn't. As I said, that would simply meant the vampaneze win. Besides," she added, her smile widening, "you aren't going to run, are you?"

"Not in a million years!" Vancha said, spitting against the wall for added emphasis. "But we won't be fools about this either. I say we check out the stadium. If it looks like Leonard's in residence, we'll force a way in and chop the fiend's head off. If not, we'll search elsewhere and the circus folk will have to make their own luck. No point risking our lives for them at this stage, aye, Darren?"

I thought of my freakish friends — Evra, Merla, Hans Hands, and the rest. I thought of Harkat and Debbie, and what might happen to them. And then I thought of my people — the vampires — and what *would* happen to the clan if we threw our lives away trying to save our non-vampire allies.

"Aye," I said miserably, and though I knew I was doing the right thing, I felt like a traitor.

Alice and Vancha checked their weapons while I armed myself with some sharp kitchen knives. Alice made a few phone calls, arranging protection for Annie and Darius. Then, with Evanna in tow, we pulled out and I left my childhood home for the second time in my life, certain in my heart that I'd never again return.

CHAPTER SIX

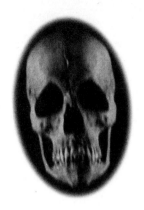

THE JOURNEY ACROSS TOWN passed without incident. All the police seemed to have been sent or drawn to the stadium. We didn't run into any roadblocks or foot patrols. In fact, we met hardly anyone. It was eerily quiet. People were in their homes or in pubs, watching the siege on TV, waiting for the action to kick off. It was a silence I knew from the past, the silence that usually comes before battle and death.

Dozens of police cars and vans were parked in a ring around the stadium when we arrived, and armed guards stood watch at every possible entry or exit point. Barriers had been erected to keep back the public and media. Ultrabright spotlights were trained on the walls of the stadium. My eyes watered from the glare of the lights, even from a long way off, and I had to stop to tie a strip of thick cloth around them.

"Are you sure you're up to this?" Alice asked, studying me doubtfully.

"I'll do what I have to," I growled, although I wasn't as convinced of my vow as I pretended to be. I was in rough shape, the roughest I'd been since my trip down the stream and through the stomach of Vampire Mountain when I'd failed my Trials of Initiation. The purge, my shoulder wound, overall exhaustion, and the blood transfer had sapped me of most of my energy. I wanted only to sleep, not face a fight to the death. But in life we don't usually get to choose the time of our defining moments. We just have to stand and face them when they come, no matter what sort of a state we're in.

A large crowd had gathered around the barriers. We mingled among them, unnoticed by the police in the darkness and crush of people — even the weirdly dressed Vancha and Evanna failed to draw attention. As we gradually pushed our way to the front, we saw thick clouds of smoke rising from within the stadium, and heard the occasional gun report.

"What's happening?" Alice asked the people nearest the barrier. "Have the police moved in?"

"Not yet," a burly man in a hunter's cap informed her. "But a small advance team went in an hour ago.

Must be some new crack unit. Most of them had shaved heads and were dressed in brown shirts and black trousers."

"Their eyes were painted red!" a young boy gasped. "I think it was blood!"

"Don't be ridiculous," his mother laughed. "That was just paint, so the glare of the lights wouldn't blind them."

We withdrew, troubled by this new information. As we were leaving, I heard the boy say, "Mommy, one of those women was dressed in ropes!"

His mother responded with a sharp, "Stop making up stories!"

"Sounds like you were right," Alice said when we were at a safe distance. "The vampets are here, and they generally don't go anywhere without their masters."

"But why did the police let them in?" I asked. "They can't be working for the vampaneze — can they?"

We looked at each other uncertainly. Vampires and vampaneze had always kept their battles private, out of the gaze of humanity. Although both sides were in the process of putting together an army of select human helpers, they'd kept the war secret from humans in general. If the vampaneze had broken that age-old custom and were working with regular human forces, it signaled a worrying new twist in the War of the Scars.

"I can still pass for a police officer," Alice said. "Wait here. I'll try to find out more about this."

She slipped forward, through the crowd and past the barrier. She was immediately challenged by a policeman, but following a quick, hushed conversation, she was led away to talk to whoever was in command.

Vancha and I waited anxiously, Evanna standing calmly nearby. I took the time to analyze my situation. I was weak, dangerously so, and my senses were going haywire. My head was pounding, and my limbs were trembling. I'd told Alice I was up for a fight, but in all honesty I couldn't say whether or not I'd be able to fend for myself. It would have been wiser to retreat and recover. But Steve had forced this battle. He was calling the shots. I'd have to struggle along as best I could and pray to the gods of the vampires for strength.

I started thinking about Evanna's prophecy again as I waited. If Vancha and I faced Steve this night, one of the three of us would die. If it was Vancha or me, Steve would become the Lord of the Shadows and the vampaneze would rule the night, as well as the world of mankind. But if Steve died, I'd become the Lord instead of him, turn on Vancha, and destroy the world.

There must be some way to change that. But how? Try to make peace with Steve? Impossible! I wouldn't even if I could, not after what he'd done to Mr. Crepsley, Tommy, Shancus, and so many others. Peace wasn't an option.

But what other way was there? I couldn't accept the fact that the world was damned. I didn't care what Evanna said. There must be a way to stop the Lord of the Shadows from rising. There *must* . . .

Alice returned ten minutes later, her features dark. "They're dancing to a vampaneze tune," she said shortly. "I pretended I was an out-of-town chief inspector. I offered my assistance. The ranking officer said they had everything under control. I asked about the brown-shirted soldiers and he told me they were a special government force. He didn't say as much, but I got the feeling he's taking orders from them. I don't know if they've bribed or threatened him, but they're pulling his strings, no doubt about it."

"So you couldn't persuade him to let us in?" Vancha asked.

"I didn't have to," Alice said. "A way's already open. One rear entrance has been left unlocked. The approaching path is being kept clear. The police around that point aren't to interfere with anyone going in."

"He told you that?" I asked, surprised.

"He was under orders to tell anyone who asked," Alice said. She spat on the ground with disgust. "Traitor!"

Vancha looked at me with a thin smile. "Leonard's in there, isn't he?"

"No doubt about it," I nodded. "He wouldn't miss something like this."

Vancha cocked a thumb at the walls of the stadium. "He's laid this on for our benefit. We're the guests of honor. Be a shame to disappoint him."

"We probably won't come out of there alive if we go in," I noted.

"That's negative thinking," Vancha tutted.

"Then we're going to proceed?" Alice asked. "We're going to push on, even though we're outnumbered and outgunned?"

"Aye," Vancha said after a moment's thought. "I'm too long in the tooth to start bothering with wisdom now!"

I grinned at my fellow Prince. Alice shrugged. Evanna remained as blank-faced as ever. Then, without discussing it any further, we slipped around back to the unguarded entrance.

The lights weren't as bright at the rear of the stadium, and there weren't many people. Lots of police were about, but they deliberately ignored us, as they'd been told to. As we were about to advance through the gap in the ranks of police, Alice stopped us. "I've had an idea," she said hesitantly. "If we all go in, they can close the net around us and we won't be able to punch our way out. But if we attack from two fronts at once . . ."

She quickly outlined her plan. It made sense to Vancha and me, so we held back while she made several phone calls. Then we waited an impatient hour, taking it easy, preparing ourselves mentally and physically. As we watched, the smoke thickened from the fires inside the stadium, and the crowd around the barriers grew. Many of the newcomers were tramps and homeless people. They mixed with the others and slowly pushed forward, where they waited close to the barriers, quiet, unnoticed.

When all was as it should be, Alice handed me a pistol and we bade her farewell. The three of us joined hands and wished each other luck. Then Vancha and I set our sights on the unguarded door. With Evanna following us like a ghost, we boldly walked past the ranks of armed police. They averted their eyes or turned their backs on us as we passed. Moments later we left the brightness outside for the darkness of the stadium tunnels and our date with destiny.

We had entered the leopard's den.

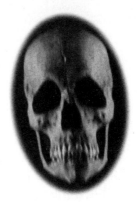

CHAPTER SEVEN

THE TUNNEL TWISTED A LOT but ran directly under the stands to the open interior of the stadium. Vancha and I walked side by side in absolute silence. If Steve was waiting, and the night went against us, one of us would die within the next few hours. There wasn't much to say in a situation like that. Vancha was probably making his peace with the vampire gods. I was worrying about what would happen after the fight, set on the idea that there must be some way to stop the coming of the Lord of the Shadows.

There were no traps along the way and we saw nobody. When we left the confines of the tunnel, we stood by the exit for a minute, numbly absorbing the chaos that Steve's troops had created. Evanna moved away slightly to our left, and she studied the carnage too.

The big top of the Cirque Du Freak, along with most of the vans and tents, had been set ablaze — the source of the bands of smoke that clogged the air overhead. The performers and circus crew had been herded together about twenty yards ahead of the tunnel, clear of the stands. Harkat stood among them, near Evra and Merla. I'd never seen his grey face filled with such rage. They were surrounded by eight armed vampets, and spotlights that had been taken from inside the big top were trained upon them. Several dead bodies lay nearby. Most were backstage crew, but one was a long-serving star of the show — the skinny, supple, musical Alexander Ribs would never take to the stage again.

Ripping the piece of cloth away from my eyes, I let my sight adjust, then looked for Debbie among the survivors — there was no sign of her. In a panic, I examined the faces and forms of the corpses again, for fear she was lying among them — but I couldn't see her.

Several vampaneze and vampets patrolled the stadium, circling the burning tents and vans, controlling the flames. As I watched, Mr. Tiny strolled out of the burning pyre of the big top, through a wall of fire, rubbing his hands together. He was wearing a red top hat and gloves — Mr. Tall's. I understood instinctively that he'd left Mr. Tall's body inside the tent, using it as a makeshift funeral pyre. Mr. Tiny didn't look upset, but I could tell by his donning of the hat and gloves that, on some level, he'd been in some way affected by his son's death.

Between the burning tent and the surviving members of the Cirque Du Freak stood a new addition — a hastily constructed gallows. Several nooses hung from the crossbeam, but only one was filled — with the poor, thin neck of the snake-boy, Shancus Von.

I cried aloud when I spotted Shancus and started to rush toward him. Vancha grabbed my left wrist and jerked me back. "We can't help him now," he growled.

"But —" I started to argue.

"Lower your gaze," he said quietly.

When I did, I saw that a band of vampaneze was grouped beneath the crossbeam and knotted ropes. All were armed with swords or battle-axes. Behind them, standing on something that raised him above them, and smirking evilly, stood their master, the Lord of the Vampaneze — Steve Leopard. He hadn't seen us yet.

"Easy," Vancha said as I stiffened. "No need to rush." His eyes were sliding slowly left and right. "How many vampaneze and vampets are here? Are there more hiding in the stands or behind the burning vans and tents? Let's work out exactly what we have to deal with before we go barging ahead."

Breathing deeply, I forced myself to think calmly, then studied the lay of the land. I counted fourteen vampaneze — nine grouped around Steve — and more than thirty vampets. I didn't see Gannen Harst, but guessed he would be close by Steve, hidden by the group of circus folk between us and the gallows.

"I make it a dozen-plus vampaneze and three times that amount of vampets, aye?" Vancha said.

"More or less," I agreed.

Vancha looked sideways at me and winked. "The odds are in our favor, Sire."

"You think so?"

"Most definitely," he said with fake enthusiasm — we both knew it didn't look good. We were vastly outnumbered by enemies with superior weapons. Our only trump card was that the vampaneze and vampets couldn't kill us. Mr. Tiny had predicted doom for them if anybody other than their Lord murdered the hunters.

Without saying anything, we started forward at the exact same moment. I was carrying two knives, one in either hand. Vancha had drawn a couple of throwing stars but was otherwise unarmed — he believed in fighting with his bare hands at close quarters. Evanna moved when we did, shadowing our every footstep.

The vampets surrounding the imprisoned Cirque

Du Freak troupe saw us coming but didn't react, except to close a little more tightly around the people they were guarding. They didn't even warn the others that we were here. Then I saw that they didn't need to — Steve and his cronies had already spotted us. Steve was standing on a box, or something, staring happily at us, while the vampaneze in front of him bunched defensively, weapons at the ready.

We had to pass the circus prisoners to get to Steve. I stopped as we drew level with Evra, Merla, and Harkat. Evra and Merla's eyes were wet with tears. Harkat's green globes were shining with fury, and he'd pulled down his mask to bare his sharp grey teeth (he could survive up to half a day without the mask).

I gazed sorrowfully at Evra and Merla, then at the body of their son, dangling from the gallows further ahead. The vampets guarding my friends watched me cautiously but made no move against me.

"Come on," Vancha said, tugging at my elbow.

"I'm sorry," I croaked to Evra and Merla, unable to continue without saying something. "I wouldn't . . . I didn't . . . if I could . . ." I stopped, unable to think of anything else to say.

Evra and Merla said nothing for a moment. Then, with a screech, Merla smashed through the guards around her and threw herself at me. "I hate you!" she screamed, scratching my face, spitting with rage. "My son's dead because of you!"

I couldn't react. I felt sick with shame. Merla dragged me to the ground, yelling and crying, beating me with her fists. The vampets moved forward to pull her off, but Steve shouted, "No! Leave them alone! This is fun!"

We rolled away from the vampets, Merla driving me back. I didn't even raise my hands to defend myself as she called me every name under the moon. I just wanted the earth to open and swallow me whole.

And then, as Merla lowered her face as though to bite me, she whispered in my ear, "Steve has Debbie." I gaped at her. She roared more insults, then whispered again, "We didn't fight. They think we're gutless, but we were waiting for *you*. Harkat said you'd come and lead us."

Merla cuffed me about the head, then locked gazes with me. "It wasn't your fault," she said, smiling ever so slightly through her tears. "We don't hate you. Steve's the evil one — not you."

"But . . . if I hadn't . . . if I'd told Vancha to kill R.V. . . ."

"Don't think that way," she snarled. "You're not to blame. Now help us kill the savages who *are*! Give us a signal when you're ready and we'll answer the call. We'll fight to the death, every last one of us."

She screamed at me again, grabbed me by the neck to strangle me, then fell off and punched the ground, sobbing pitifully. Evra pushed forward, collected his wife, and led her back to the pack. He glanced at me once, fleetingly, and I saw the same thing in his expression that I'd seen in Merla's — sorrow for the loss of their son, hatred for Steve and his gang, but only pity for me.

I still felt at fault for what had happened to Shancus and the others. But Evra and Merla's sympathy gave me the strength to carry on. If they'd hated me, I doubt I could have continued. But now that they'd given me their backing, I not only felt able to push on — I felt that I had to. For their sakes, if not my own.

I got to my feet, acting shaken. As Vancha came to help me, I spoke quickly and quietly. "They're with us. They'll fight when we do."

He paused, then carried on as though I hadn't spoken, checking my face where Merla had scratched me, loudly asking if she'd harmed me, if I was OK, if I wanted to rest awhile.

"I'm fine," I grunted, pushing past him, showing my circus friends a stiff back, as if they'd insulted me.

"Merla said Steve has Debbie," I hissed to Vancha out of the side of my mouth, barely moving my lips.

"We might not be able to save her," he whispered back.

"I know," I said stonily. "But we'll try?"

A short pause. Then, "Aye," he replied.

With that, we quickened our pace and made a bee-line for the gallows and the grinning, demonic, half-vampaneze beast waiting underneath, face half hidden by the shadow of the dangling Shancus Von.

CHAPTER EIGHT

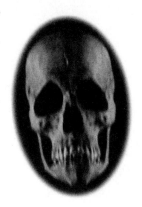

"**H**ALT!" ONE OF THE NINE vampaneze in front of Steve shouted when we were about five yards away. We stopped. This close, I saw that Steve was actually standing on the body of one of the circus crew — Pasta O'Malley, a man who used to sleepwalk and even sleep-read. I could also see Gannen Harst now, just to Steve's right, sword undrawn, watching us intently.

"Drop your throwing stars," the vampaneze said to Vancha. When he didn't respond, two of the vampaneze raised spears and pointed them at him. With a shrug, Vancha slid the shurikens back into their holders and lowered his hands.

I glanced up at Shancus, swinging in the light breeze. The crossbeam creaked. The sound was louder than normal for me because of the purge — like the squeal of a wild boar.

"Get him down," I snarled at Steve.

"I don't think so," Steve replied lightly. "I like the sight of him up there. Maybe I'll hang his parents beside him. His brother and sister too. Keep the whole family together. What do you think?"

"Why do you go along with this madman?" Vancha asked Gannen Harst. "I don't care what Des Tiny says about him — this lunatic can bring nothing but shame upon the vampaneze. You should have killed him years ago."

"He is of our blood," Gannen Harst replied quietly. "I don't agree with his ways — he knows that — but we don't kill our kin."

"You do if they break your laws," Vancha grunted. "Leonard lies and uses guns. Any normal vampaneze would be executed if they did that."

"But he isn't normal," Gannen said. "He is our Lord. Desmond Tiny said we would perish if we did not follow him and obey. Whether I like it or not, Steve has the power to bend our laws, or even ignore them completely. I'd rather he didn't, but it's not my place to chastise him when he does."

"You can't approve of his actions," Vancha pushed.

"No," Gannen admitted. "But he has been accepted by the clan, and I am only a servant of my people. History can judge Steve. I'm content to serve and protect, in line with the wishes of those who appointed me."

Vancha glared at his brother, trying to stare him down, but Gannen only gazed back blankly. Then Steve laughed. "Aren't family get-togethers a joy?" he said. "I was hoping you'd bring Annie and Darius along. Imagine the fun all six of us could have had!"

"They're far away from here by now," I said. I wanted to dive for him and rip his throat open with my bare hands and teeth, but his guards would have cut me down before I struck. I had to be patient and pray for a chance to present itself.

"How's my son?" Steve asked. "Did you kill him?"

"Of course not," I snorted. "I didn't have to. When he saw you murder Shancus he realized you were a monster. I filled him in on your past 'glories.' Annie told him some old stories too. He'll never listen to you again. You've lost him. He's your son no more."

I hoped to wound Steve with my words but he just laughed them off. "Oh well, I was never that fond of him anyway. A scrawny, moody kid. No taste for blood. Although," he chuckled, "I guess he'll develop one soon!"

"I wouldn't be too sure of that," I retorted.

"I blooded him," Steve boasted. "He's half-vampaneze."

"No," I smiled. "He's a half-vampire. Like me."

Steve stared at me uncertainly. "You re-blooded him?"

"Yes. He's one of us now. He won't need to kill when he feeds. Like I said, he's no longer your son — in any way whatsoever."

Steve's features darkened. "You shouldn't have done that," he growled. "The boy was mine."

"He was never yours, not in spirit," I said. "You merely tricked him into believing he was."

Steve started to reply, then scowled and shook his head gruffly. "Never mind," he muttered. "The child's not important. I'll deal with him — and his mother — later. Let's get down to the good stuff. We all know the prophecy." He nodded at Mr. Tiny, who was wandering around the burning tents and vans, paying no apparent interest to us. "Darren or Vancha will kill me, or I'll kill one of you, and that will decide the fate of the War of the Scars."

"If Tiny's right, or telling the truth, aye," Vancha sniffed.

"You don't believe him?" Steve frowned.

"Not entirely," Vancha said. "Tiny and his daughter" — he glared at Evanna — "have agendas of their own. I accept most of what they predict, but I don't treat their predictions as absolute facts."

"Then why are you here?" Steve challenged him.

"In case they *are* correct."

Steve looked confused. "How can you not believe them? Desmond Tiny is the voice of destiny. He sees the future. He knows all that has been and will be."

"We make our own futures," Vancha said. "Regardless of what happens tonight, I believe my people will defeat yours. But I'll kill you anyway," he added with a wicked grin. "Just to be on the safe side."

"You're an ignorant fool," Steve said, shaking with outrage. Then his gaze settled on me. "I bet *you* believe the prophecy."

"Maybe," I replied.

"Of course you do," Steve smiled. "And you know it's you or me, don't you? Vancha's a red herring. You and I are the sons of destiny, the ruler and slave, the victor and vanquished. Leave Vancha behind, step up here alone, and I swear it will be a fair fight. You and me, man to man, one winner, one loser. A Vampaneze Lord to rule the night — or a Vampire Prince."

"How can I trust you?" I asked. "You're a liar. You'll spring a trap."

"No," Steve barked. "You have my word."

"Like that means anything," I jeered, but I could

see an eagerness in Steve's expression. His offer was genuine. I glanced sideways at Vancha. "What do you think?"

"No," Vancha said. "We're in this together. We'll take him on as a team."

"But if he's prepared to fight me fairly . . ."

"That demon knows nothing about fairness," Vancha said. "He'd cheat — that's his nature. We'll do nothing the way he wants."

"Very well." I faced Steve again. "Stuff your offer. What next?"

I thought Steve was going to leap over the ranks of vampaneze and attack me. He gnashed his teeth, hands twisted together, shivering furiously. Gannen Harst saw it too, but to my surprise, rather than step in to calm Steve down, he took a half-step back. It was as if he wanted Steve to leap, like he'd had enough of his insane, evil Lord, and wanted this matter settled, one way or the other.

But just when it seemed as if the moment of final confrontation had come, Steve relaxed and his smile returned. "I do my best," he sighed. "I try to make it easy for everybody, but some people are determined not to play ball. Very well. Here's 'what next'."

Steve put his fingers to his lips and whistled sharply.

From behind the gallows, R.V. stepped out. The bearded, ex-eco-warrior was holding a rope between three lonely-looking hooks (Mr. Tall had snapped the other hooks off before he died). When he tugged on the rope, a bound woman shuffled out after him — Debbie.

I'd been expecting this, so I didn't panic. R.V. walked Debbie forward a few paces but stopped a long way short of Steve. The one-time campaigner for peace and the protection of mother nature didn't look very happy. He was twitchy, head jerking, eyes unfocused, nervously chewing at his lower lip, which was bleeding from where he'd bitten through the flesh. R.V. had been a proud, earnest, dedicated man when I first met him, fighting to save the world from pollution. Then he'd become a mad beast, intent only on gaining revenge for the loss of his hands. Now he was neither — just a ragged, sorry mess.

Steve didn't notice R.V.'s confusion. He had eyes only for Debbie. "Isn't she beautiful?" he mocked me. "Like an angel. More warrior-like than the last time we met, but all the lovelier because of it." He looked at me slyly. "Be a shame if I had to tell R.V. to gut her like a rabid dog."

"You can't use her against me," I said softly, gazing at Steve without blinking. "She knows who you are and what's at stake. I love her, but my first duty is to my clan. She understands that."

"You mean you'll stand there and let her die?" Steve shrieked.

"Yes!" Debbie shouted before I could reply.

"You people," Steve groaned. "You're determined to annoy me. I try to be fair, but you toss it back in my face and . . ." He hopped off Pasta O'Malley's back and ranted and raved, striding up and down behind his guards. I kept a close watch on him. If he stepped out too far, I'd strike. But even in his rage he was careful not to expose himself.

All of a sudden Steve stopped. "So be it!" he snarled. "R.V. — kill her!"

R.V. didn't respond. He was gazing miserably down at the ground.

"R.V.!" Steve shouted. "Didn't you hear me? Kill her!"

"Don't want to," R.V. mumbled. His eyes came up and I saw pain and doubt in them. "You shouldn't have killed the kid, Steve. He did nothing to hurt us. It was wrong. Kids are the future, man."

"I did what I had to," Steve replied tightly. "Now you'll do the same."

"But she's not a vampire . . ."

"She works for them!" Steve shouted.

"I know," R.V. moaned. "But why do we have to kill her? Why did you kill the kid? It was Darren we were meant to kill. *He's* the enemy, man. He's the one who cost me my hands."

"Don't betray me now," Steve growled, stepping toward the bearded vampaneze. "You've killed people too, the innocent as well as the guilty. Don't get moralistic on me. It doesn't become you."

"But . . . but . . . but . . ."

"Stop stuttering and kill her!" Steve screamed. He took another step forward and moved clear of his guards without being aware of it. I steeled myself to make a dash at him, but Vancha was one move ahead of me.

"Now!" Vancha roared, leaping forward, drawing a shuriken and launching it at Steve. He would have killed him, except the guard at the end of the line saw the danger just in time and threw himself into the path of the deadly throwing star, sacrificing himself to save his Lord.

As the other guards surged sideways to block Vancha's path to their Lord, I sheathed my knives, drew the pistol I'd borrowed from Alice before entering the stadium, aimed it at the sky, and pulled the trigger three times — the signal for all-out riot!

CHAPTER NINE

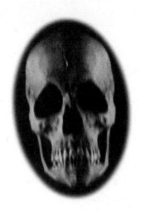

Even before the echoes of the report of my third shot faded, the air outside the stadium filled with answering gunfire, as Alice and her band of vampirites opened fire on the police standing guard. She'd summoned the homeless people before Vancha and I entered the tunnel, and positioned them around the barrier outside the stadium. After years of surviving on the scraps other people threw away, this was their time to rise. They had only a small amount of training and basic weapons, but they had passion and anger on their side, and the desire to prove themselves. So now, at my signal, they leaped the barriers around the stadium and attacked as a unified force, throwing themselves upon the startled police, sacrificing themselves where necessary, fighting and dying not just for their own lives, but for the lives of those who considered them trash.

We weren't sure of the intentions of the police. Steve might have told them to remain outside regardless of what happened inside, in which case the attack by the vampirites would serve no purpose at all. But if they were there to support the vampaneze and vampets, to come to their aid if summoned, the vampirites could divert them and buy those of us inside the stadium a bit more space and time.

Most of the vampaneze guarding Steve moved to stop Vancha when he charged, but two lunged at me as I fired the pistol. They tackled me to the ground, knocking the gun from my hand. I struck out at them but they simply lay on top of me, pinning me down. They would have held me there, helpless, while their colleagues dealt with Vancha. Except . . .

The stars and crew of the Cirque Du Freak had also rallied to my signal. At the same time that the vampirites attacked the police, the prisoners inside the stadium turned on the vampets holding them captive. They attacked with their bare hands, driving the vampets back by sheer force of numbers. The vampets fired into the crowd and hacked wildly with their swords and axes. Several people fell, dead or wounded. But the group pushed on regardless, screaming, punching, kicking, biting — no force on Earth could hold them back.

While the bulk of the Cirque Du Freak troupe grappled with the vampets, Harkat led a small band toward the gallows. He'd grabbed an ax from a dead vampet, and with one smooth swing he cut down a vampaneze who tried to intercept them, rushing past without breaking his stride.

Vancha was still locked in a struggle with Steve's guards, doing his best to break through to their Lord. He'd downed two of them but the others were standing firm. He was cut in many places, knife and spear wounds, but none fatal. Looking around, I saw Gannen Harst push Steve away from the threat. Steve was arguing with him — he wanted to take Vancha on.

Behind Steve and Gannen Harst, R.V. had let go of Debbie's rope and was backing away from her, shaking his head, hooks crossed behind his back, wanting no part of this. Debbie was tugging at her bonds, trying to wriggle free.

The two vampaneze holding me down saw Harkat and others racing toward them. Cursing, they abandoned me and lashed out at their attackers. They were too swift for the ordinary circus folk — three died quickly — but Truska was part of the group, and she wasn't so easily done away with. She'd let her beard grow while she'd been waiting to fight — the unnatural blond hair now trailed down past her feet. Standing back, she made the beard rise — she could control the hairs as though they were snakes — then directed the twisting strands toward one of the vampaneze. The beard parted into two prongs, then curled around the startled vampaneze's throat and tightened. He sliced at the hair and at Truska, but she had him too firmly in her grip. He fell to his knees, purple features darkening even further as he choked.

Harkat took on the other vampaneze, chopping at him with his ax. The Little Person lacked the speed of a vampaneze, but he was very powerful and his round green eyes were alert to his opponent's swift moves. He could fight as an equal, as he had many times in the past.

I circled around the vampaneze struggling with Vancha. I meant to go after Steve, but he and Gannen had linked up with three of the vampaneze who'd been roaming the grounds of the stadium. I didn't like the five-to-one odds, so I went to cut Debbie free instead.

"They surrounded the stadium shortly after Harkat and I arrived," she cried as I sliced through the ropes binding her arms. "I tried calling, but it wouldn't work. It was Mr. Tiny. He blocked my signal. I saw his watch glowing, and he was laughing."

"It's OK," I said. "We'd have come anyway. We had to."

"Is that Alice outside?" Debbie asked. The gunfire was deafening now.

"Yes," I said. "The vampirites seem to be enjoying their first taste of action."

Vancha lurched over to us, streaming blood. The vampaneze had given up on him and retreated, teaming up with the vampets and picking fights with the circus folk. "Where's Leonard?" Vancha bellowed.

I peered around the stadium but it was almost impossible to pick out any individuals in the press of bodies. "I had him in my sights a minute ago," I said. "He must be here somewhere."

"Not if Gannen flitted with him!" Vancha roared. He wiped blood clear of his eyes and looked for Steve and Gannen again.

"Are you badly wounded?" Debbie asked him.

"Scratches!" Vancha grunted. Then he shouted, "There! Behind the fat man!"

He rushed forward, bellowing madly. Squinting, I caught a glimpse of Steve. He was close to the enormous Rhamus Twobellies, warily backing away from him. Rhamus was literally falling on his opponents, squashing them lifeless.

Debbie darted away from me, picked the bodies of

the dead vampaneze clean of their weapons, and returned with an array of knives and two swords. She gave one of the swords to me and hefted the other herself. It was too large for her, but she held it steady, face set. "You go get Steve," she said. "I'll help the others."

"Be —" I began, but she'd already raced out of earshot, "— careful," I finished softly. I shook my head, smiled briefly, then set off after Steve.

Around me the battle was raging. The circus folk were locked in bloody combat with the vampets and vampaneze, fighting clumsily but effectively, blind fury compensating for lack of military training. The gifted freaks were a huge help. Truska was causing havoc with her beard. Rhamus was an immovable foe. Gertha Teeth was biting off fingers, noses, sword tips. Hans Hands had tucked his legs behind his neck and was dodging between the enemy forces on his hands, too low for them to easily strike, tripping them up and dividing them.

Vancha had come to a halt, held up by the fighting. He started firing shurikens at those enemies ahead of him, to clear a path. Jekkus Flang stepped up beside him and added his throwing knives to Vancha's stars. A deadly, efficient combination. I couldn't help thinking what a great show they could have put on if we'd been playing to an audience tonight instead of fighting for our lives.

Mr. Tiny was picking his way through the mass of warring bodies, beaming merrily, admiring the corpses of the dead, studying the dying with polite interest, applauding those locked in especially vicious duels. Evanna was edging toward her father, uninterested in the carnage, bare feet and lower ropes stained with blood.

Gannen and Steve were still backing away from the massive Rhamus Twobellies, using him as a shield — it was hard for anybody else to get at them with Rhamus in the way. I tracked them like a hound, closing in. I was almost at the mouth of the tunnel through which we'd entered the stadium when fresh bodies burst through it. My insides tightened — I thought the police had come to the aid of their companions, meaning almost certain defeat for us. But then, to my astonished delight, I realized it was Alice Burgess and a dozen or so vampirites. Declan and Little Kenny — the pair who'd rescued me from the street when Darius shot me — were among them.

"Still alive?" Alice shouted as her troops laid into the vampaneze and vampets, faces twisted with excitement and battle lust.

"How'd you get in?" I yelled in reply. The plan had

been for her to cause a diversion outside the stadium, to hold up the police — not invade with a force of her own.

"We attacked at the front, as planned," she said. "The police rushed to that point, to battle *en masse* — they lack discipline. Most of my troops fled with the crowd after a few minutes — you should have seen the chaos! — but I slipped around the back with a few volunteers. The entrance to the tunnel is completely unguarded now. We —"

A vampet attacked her, and she had to wheel aside to deal with him. I did a very quick head count. With the addition of the vampirites, we seriously outnumbered the vampaneze and vampets. Although the fighting was brutal and disorganized, we had the upper hand. Unless the police outside recovered swiftly and rushed in, we'd win this battle! But that would mean nothing if Steve escaped, so I put all thoughts of victory on hold and went in pursuit of him again.

I didn't get very far. R.V. had backed away from the fighting. He was heading for the tunnel, but I was standing almost directly in his path. When he saw me, he stopped. I wasn't sure what to do — fight or let him escape so that I could go after Steve? While I was making up my mind, Cormac Limbs stepped in between us.

"Come on, hairy!" he roared at R.V., slapping his

face with his left hand, jabbing at him with a knife held in his right. "Let's see what you're made of!"

"No!" R.V. moaned. "I don't want to fight."

"The devil you don't, you big, bearded, bug-eyed baboon!" Cormac shouted, slapping R.V. again. This time R.V. lashed out at Cormac's hand with his hooks. He cut two of the fingers off, but they immediately grew back. "You'll have to do better than that, stink-breath!" Cormac taunted him.

"Then I will!" R.V. shouted, losing his cool. Jumping forward, he knocked Cormac over, knelt on his chest, and before I could do anything, he struck at Cormac's neck with his hooks. He didn't cut it clean off, but sliced about halfway through. Then, with a grunt, he hacked through the rest of it, and tossed Cormac's head aside like a ball.

"You shouldn't have messed with me, man!" R.V. groaned, rising shakily. I was about to attack him, to avenge Cormac's death, but then I saw that he was sobbing. "I didn't want to kill you!" R.V. howled. "I didn't want to kill anybody! I wanted to help people. I wanted to save the world. I . . ."

He ground to a halt, eyes widening with disbelief. Glancing down, I also came to a stunned stop. Where Cormac's head had been, two new heads were growing, shooting out on a pair of thin necks. They were slightly smaller than his old head, but otherwise identical. When they stopped growing, there was a short pause. Then Cormac's eyes fluttered open and he spat blood out of both mouths. His eyes came into focus. He looked at R.V. with one set and at me with the other. Then his heads turned and he stared at himself.

"So that's what happens when I cut my head off!" he exclaimed through both mouths at the same time. "I always wondered about that!"

"Madness!" R.V. screamed. "The world's gone mad! *Mad!*"

Spinning crazily, he rushed past Cormac, then past me, gibbering insanely, drooling, and falling over. I could have killed him easily — but I chose not to. Standing aside, I let the wretch pass, and watched sadly as he staggered down the tunnel, out of sight. R.V. had never been right in the head since losing his hands, and now he'd lost his senses completely. I couldn't bring myself to punish this pathetic shadow of a man.

And now, at last — Steve. He and Gannen were part of a small band of vampaneze and vampets. They'd been forced toward the center of the stadium by the freaks, circus helpers, and vampirites. Lots of smaller fights were still being waged around the stadium, but this was their last big stand. If this unit fell, they were all doomed.

Vancha was closing in on the group. I joined him. There was no sign of Jekkus Flang — I didn't know whether he'd fallen to the enemy or run out of knives, and this wasn't the time to ask questions. Vancha paused when he saw me. "Ready?" he asked.

"Ready," I said.

"I don't care which of us kills him," Vancha said, "but let me go first. If —" He stopped, face twisting with fear. "No!" he roared.

Following the direction of his eyes, I saw that Steve had tripped. Evra stood over him, a long knife held in both hands, determined to take the life of the man who'd killed his son. If he struck, the Lord of the Vampaneze would die by the hand of one who wasn't destined to kill him. If Mr. Tiny's prophecy was true, that would have dire results for the vampire clan.

As we watched, unable to prevent it, Evra stopped abruptly. He shook his head, blinked dumbly — then stepped over Steve and left him lying on the ground, unharmed. Steve sat up, bleary-eyed, not sure what had happened. Gannen Harst stooped and helped him to his feet. The two men stood, alone in the crush, totally ignored by everyone around them.

"Over there," I whispered, touching Vancha's shoulder. Far off to our right, Mr. Tiny stood, eyes on Steve and Gannen. He was holding his heart-shaped watch in his right hand. It was glowing redly. Evanna was standing beside him, her face illuminated by the glow of her father's watch.

I don't know if Steve and Gannen saw Mr. Tiny and realized that he was protecting them. But they were alert enough to seize their chance and run for the freedom of the tunnel.

Mr. Tiny watched the pair race free of danger. Then he looked at Vancha and me, and smiled. The glow of his watch faded and his lips moved softly. Even though we were a long way off, we heard him clearly, as if he was standing next to us. "It's time, boys!"

"Harkat!" I shouted, wanting him to come with us, to be there at the end, as he'd been by my side for so much of the hunt. But he didn't hear me. Nobody did. I glanced around the stadium at Harkat, Alice, Evra, Debbie. All of my friends were locked in battle with the vampaneze and vampets. None of them knew what was happening with Steve and Gannen Harst. They weren't part of this. It was just me and Vancha now.

"To the death, Sire?" Vancha murmured.

"To the death," I agreed miserably. I ran my eyes over the faces of my friends for what might be the final time, bidding silent farewells to the scaly Evra Von, the grey-skinned Harkat Mulds, the steely Alice Burgess, and my beloved Debbie Hemlock, more beautiful than ever as she tore into her foes like an Amazonian warrior of old. Perhaps it was for the best that I couldn't bid them a proper farewell. There was so much to say, I don't know where I would have begun.

Then Vancha and I jogged after Steve and Gannen Harst, not rushing, sure that they wouldn't flit, not this time, not until we'd satisfied the terms of Mr. Tiny's prophecy and Steve or one of us lay dead. Behind us, Mr. Tiny and Evanna followed like ghosts. They alone would bear witness to the final battle, the death of one of the hunters or Steve — and the birth of the Lord of the Shadows, destroyer of the present and all-ruling monster of the future.

CHAPTER TEN

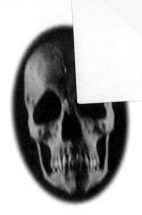

WE FOLLOWED STEVE AND GANNEN down the hill at the rear of the stadium. They were fleeing toward the river, but they weren't racing at top speed. Either one of them was injured or, like ourselves, they'd simply accepted the fact that we had to fight, an evenly matched contest, to the bitter, bloody end.

As we jogged down the hill, leaving the stadium, lights, and noises behind, my headache lessened. I would have been glad of that, except now that I was able to focus, I realized how physically drained I was. I'd been operating on reserve energy for a long time and had just about run dry. Even the simplest movement was a huge chore. All I could do was carry on as long as possible and hope I got an adrenaline burst when we caught up with our prey.

As we reached level ground at the bottom of the hill, I stumbled and almost fell. Luckily Vancha had been keeping an eye on me. He caught and steadied me. "Feel bad?" he asked.

"Awful," I groaned.

"Maybe you're not meant to go any further," he said. "Perhaps you should rest here and —"

"Save your breath," I stopped him. "I'm going on, even if I have to crawl."

Vancha laughed, then tilted my head back and examined my face, his small eyes unusually dark. "You'll make a fine vampire," he said. "I hope I'm around to celebrate your coming of age."

"You're not getting defeatist on me, are you?" I grunted.

"No." He smiled weakly. "We'll win. Of course we will. I just . . ."

He stopped, slapped my back, and urged me on. Wearily, every step an effort, I threw myself after Steve and Gannen Harst again. I did my best to match Vancha's pace, swinging my legs as evenly as I could, keeping the rest of my body limp, relaxed, saving energy.

Steve and Gannen reached the river and turned right, jogging along the bank. As they came to the arch of a bridge spanning the river, they stopped. It looked like they were having an argument. Gannen was trying to pick Steve up — I assumed he meant to flit, with Steve on his back, as they'd escaped from us once before. Steve was having none of it. He slapped his protector's hands away, gesturing furiously. Then, as we closed upon them, Gannen's shoulders sagged and he nodded wearily. The pair turned away from the pass beneath the bridge, drew their weapons, and stood waiting for us.

We slowed and walked the rest of the way. I could hear Mr. Tiny and Evanna close behind — they'd caught up to us within the last few seconds — but I didn't turn to look back.

"You could use your shurikens," I whispered to Vancha as we came within range of Steve and Gannen Harst.

"That would be dishonorable," Vancha replied. "They've faced us openly, in expectations of a fair fight. We must confront them."

He was right. Killing mercilessly wasn't the vampire way. But I half wished he'd put his principles aside, for once, and fire his throwing stars at them until they dropped. It would be much simpler and surer that way.

We drew to a halt a couple of yards short of Steve and Gannen. Steve's eyes were alight with excitement and a slight shade of fear — he knew there were no guarantees now, no more opportunities for dirty tricks or games. It was a plain, fair fight to the death, and that was something he couldn't control.

"Greetings, brother," Gannen Harst said, bowing his head.

"Greetings," Vancha replied stiffly. "I'm glad you face us like true creatures of the night at last. Perhaps in death you can find again the honor that you abandoned during life."

"Honor will be shared by all here tonight," Gannen said, "both the living and the dead."

"They love talking," Steve sighed. He squared up to me. "Ready to die, Shan?"

I stepped forward. "If that's what fate has in store for me — yes," I answered. "But I'm also ready to kill." With that I raised my sword and struck the first blow of the fight that would decide the outcome of the War of the Scars.

Steve stood his ground, brought his own sword up — it was shorter and easier to handle than mine — and turned my blow aside. Gannen Harst stabbed at me with his long, straight sword. Vancha slapped the blade wide of its target and pulled me out of immediate range of his brother.

Vancha only gave me a relatively gentle tug, but in my weakened state I staggered backward and wound up in an untidy mess on the ground, close to Mr. Tiny and Evanna. By the time I struggled to my feet, Vancha was locked in combat with Steve and Gannen Harst, hands a blur as he defended himself against their swords with his bare palms.

"He's a fierce creature, isn't he?" Mr. Tiny remarked to his daughter. "Quite the beast of nature. I like him."

Evanna didn't reply. All her senses were focused on the battle, and there was worry and uncertainty in her eyes. I knew in that moment that she'd told the truth and really didn't know which way this would go.

I turned away from the onlookers and caught quick flashes of the fight that was unfolding at superhuman speed. Steve nicked Vancha's left arm near the top — Vancha kicked him in the chest in return. Gannen's sword scraped down Vancha's left side, slicing a thin gouge from breast to waist — Vancha replied by grabbing his brother's sword hand and wrenching it back, snapping the bones of his wrist. Gannen gasped with pain as he dropped the sword, then ducked for it and grabbed it with his left hand. As he came to his feet again, Vancha struck his head with his right knee. Gannen fell away with a heavy grunt.

Vancha spun around to deal with Steve, but Steve was already upon him, making short sweeps with his sword, keeping Vancha at bay. Vancha tried to grab the sword, but only succeeded in having the flesh of his palms cut open. I staggered up beside him. I wasn't of much use right then — I could barely raise my sword, and my legs dragged like dead weights — but at least it provided Steve with a double threat. If I could distract him, Vancha might be able to penetrate his defenses and strike.

As I drew level with Vancha, panting and sweating, Gannen swung back into battle, dazed but determined, chopping angrily at Vancha, forcing him to retreat. I stabbed at Gannen, but Steve deflected my sword with his, then let go of the handle with one hand and punched me between the eyes. I dropped back, startled, and Steve drove the tip of his sword at my face.

If he'd had both hands on the sword, he'd have thrust it through me. But one-handed, he wasn't able to direct it as powerfully as he wished. I managed to knock it aside with my left arm. A deep cut opened up just below my elbow, and I felt all the strength leave the fingers of that hand.

Steve stabbed at me again. I raised my sword to protect myself. Too late I realized he'd only feinted. Wheeling around, he threw himself into me, right shoulder first. He struck me heavily in the chest and I fell back, winded, losing hold of my sword. There was a yell behind me and I crashed into Vancha. Both of us went down, Vancha taken by surprise, arms and legs entangled with mine.

It took Vancha no more than a second to free himself — but that second was all Gannen Harst required. Darting forward, almost too fast for me to see, he stuck the tip of his sword into the small of Vancha's back — then shoved it all the way through and out the front of Vancha's stomach!

Vancha's eyes and mouth shot wide open. Gannen stood behind him a moment. Then he stepped away and pulled his sword free. Blood gushed out of Vancha, both in front and behind, and he collapsed in agony, face twisted, limbs thrashing.

"May your gods forgive me, brother," Gannen whispered, his face haggard, eyes haunted. "Though I fear I'll never forgive myself."

I scrambled away from the downed Prince, chasing my sword. Steve stood close by, laughing. With an effort, Gannen regained control and set about securing victory. Hurrying over to me, he stood on my sword so that I couldn't lift it, sheathed his own blade, and grabbed my head with his good left hand. "Hurry!" he barked at Steve. "Kill him quick!"

"What's the rush?" Steve muttered.

"If Vancha dies of the wound I gave him, we'll have broken the rules of Mr. Tiny's prophecy!" Gannen shouted.

Steve pulled a face. "Bloody prophecies," he grumbled. "Maybe I'll let him die and see what happens. Maybe I don't care about Tiny or . . ." He stopped and rolled his eyes. "Oh, how *silly* we are! The answer's obvious — *I'll* kill Vancha before he dies of your wound. That way we'll fulfill the requirements of the stupid prophecy *and* I'll get to hang on to Darren, so I can torture him later."

"Clever boy," I heard Mr. Tiny murmur.

"Have it any way you wish!" Gannen roared. "But if you're going to kill him, kill him now, so that —"

"*No!*" someone screamed. Before anyone could react, a large shape shot out of the underpass beneath the bridge and hurled itself at Gannen, knocking him off me, almost toppling him into the river. Sitting up, I got a shocked fix on my most unlikely of rescuers — *R.V.!*

"Not gonna let you do it, man!" R.V. screamed, pounding Gannen Harst with his hooks. "You're evil!"

Gannen had been taken completely unaware, but he swiftly recovered, fumbled his sword free of its scabbard, and dug at R.V. with it. R.V. caught the sword with his gold right-handed hooks and smashed it against the ground, snapping it in two. With a roar of triumph, he slammed his silver left-handed hook into the side of Gannen's head. There was a crack, and Gannen's eyes went blank. He slumped beneath R.V., unconscious. R.V. howled with joy, then drew both arms back to bring them down sharply and finish Gannen off.

Before R.V. could strike, Steve stepped up behind him and forced a knife up beneath his bushy beard, deep into his throat. R.V. shuddered and bowled Steve over. R.V. stood, spinning crazily, grabbing for the handle of the knife with his hooks. After missing it several times, he fell down, landing on his knees, head thrown back.

R.V. knelt there a moment, swaying sickeningly. Then his arms slowly rose. He gazed at the gold and silver hooks, his face glowing with wonder. "My hands," he said softly, and although his voice was gurgly with blood, his words were clear. "I can see them. My hands. They're back. Everything's OK now. I'm normal again, man." Then his arms dropped, his smile and pale red eyes froze in place, and his soul passed quietly on to the next world.

CHAPTER ELEVEN

I GAZED AT R.V.'S PEACEFUL EXPRESSION as he knelt in his death pose. He'd left his pain behind at last, forever. I was glad for him. If he'd lived, he'd have had to carry around the memory of the evil he'd committed while in league with the vampaneze. Maybe he was better off this way.

"And now there's two — just me and you," Steve trilled, breaking my train of thought. I glanced up and saw him standing a few yards away from R.V., smiling. Gannen Harst was still out for the count, and although Vancha was alive, he was lying motionless, wheezing fitfully, unable to defend himself or attack.

"Yes," I agreed, standing and picking up my sword. My left hand wouldn't work, and my system was maybe a minute or two away from complete shutdown. But I had enough strength left for one last fight.

First, though — Vancha. I paused over him and studied his wound. It was seeping blood, and his face was creased with pain. He tried to speak, but words wouldn't form.

As I hovered uncertainly by the side of my fellow Prince, unwilling to leave him like this, Evanna crossed to his side, knelt, and examined him. Her eyes were grave when she looked up. "It is not fatal," she said softly. "He will live."

"Thank you," I muttered.

"Save your thanks," Mr. Tiny said. He was standing directly behind me. "She didn't tell you to cheer you up, silly boy. It was a warning. Vancha won't die for the time being, but he's out of the fight. You're alone. The final hunter. Unless you turn tail and run, it's down to you and Steve now. If Steve doesn't die, death will come within the next few minutes for *you*."

I looked over my shoulder at the small man in the yellow suit and green rain boots. His face was bright with bloodthirsty glee. "If death comes," I said shortly, "it will be a far more welcome companion than you."

Mr. Tiny chuckled, then stepped away to my left. Rising, Evanna took up position on my right. Both waited for me to move, so that they could follow. I spared Vancha one final glance — he grinned painfully at me and winked — then faced Steve.

He backed away from me casually, entering the

shadows beneath the bridge. I trailed after him, sword by my side, taking deep breaths, clearing my mind, focusing on the death-struggle to come. Although this could have been Vancha's battle, a part of me had known all along that it would come down to this. Steve and I were opposite sides of a coin, linked since childhood, first by friendship, then hatred. It was only fitting that the final confrontation should fall to the two of us.

I entered the cool darkness of the underpass. It took my eyes a few seconds to adjust. When they did, I saw Steve waiting, right eye twitching nervously. The river gurgled softly beside us, the only noise except for our panting and chattering teeth.

"There is where we settle matters, once and for all, in the dark," Steve said.

"As good a place as any," I replied.

Steve raised his left palm. I could vaguely make out the shape of the pink cross he'd carved into his flesh eighteen years before. "Remember when I did this?" he asked. "That night, I swore I'd kill you and Creepy Crepsley."

"You're halfway there," I noted drily. "You must be delighted."

"Not really," he said. "To be honest, I miss old Creepy. The world's not the same without him. I'll miss you even more. You've been the driving force behind everything I've done since I was a child. Without you, I'm not sure I'll have much of an interest in life. If possible, I'd let you go. I enjoy our games — the hunt, the traps, the fights. I'd happily keep doing it, over and over, a new twist here, a fresh shock there."

"But life doesn't work like that," I said. "Everything has to end."

"Yes," Steve said sadly. "That's one thing I can't change." His mood passed and he regarded me with a sneer. "Here's where *you* end, Darren Shan. This is your grand finale. Have you made your peace with the vampire gods?"

"I'll do that later," I snarled, and swung my sword wide, moving forward so that on its return arc he'd be within range. But before it had completed its first arc, the tip of the sword smashed into the wall. It bounced off in a shower of sparks, and a shock ran down my arm.

"Silly boy," Steve purred, mimicking Mr. Tiny. He raised a knife. "No room here for swords."

Steve leaped and jabbed the knife at me. I pulled back and lobbed my sword at him, momentarily halting him. In that second, I drew one of the knives I'd brought from Annie's kitchen. When Steve advanced, I was ready. I caught his thrust with the hilt of my knife and turned his blade aside.

There was no room in the underpass to circle one

another, so we had to jab and stab, ducking and weaving to avoid each other's blows. The conditions actually played in my favor — in the open I'd have had to be nimbler on my feet, spinning to keep up with Steve. That would have exhausted me. Here, since we were so cramped, I could stand still and direct my rapidly dwindling strength into my knife hand.

We fought silently, fast, sharp, impulsive. Steve nicked the flesh of my forearm — I nicked his. He opened shallow wounds on my stomach and chest — I repaid the compliment. He almost cut my nose off — I nearly severed his left ear.

Then Steve came at me from the left, taking advantage of my dead arm. He grabbed the material of my shirt and pulled me toward him, driving his knife hard at my belly with his other hand. I rolled with the force of his pull, throwing myself into him. His knife cut the wall of my stomach, a deep wound, but my momentum carried me forward despite the pain. I drove him down, landing awkwardly on him as he hit the path. His right hand flew out by his side, fingers snapping open. His knife shot free and struck the river with a splash, vanishing from sight in an instant.

Steve brought his empty right hand up, to push me off. I stabbed at it with my knife and hit home, spearing him through his forearm. He screamed. I freed my knife before he could knock it from my grip, raised it to shoulder height, and redirected it, so the tip was pointing at Steve's throat. His eyes shot to the gleam of the blade and his breath caught. This was it. I had him. He'd been out-fought and he knew it. One quick thrust of the knife and —

Searing pain. A white flash inside my head. I thought Gannen had recovered and struck me from behind, but he hadn't. It was an aftershock from when I blooded Darius. Vancha had warned me about this. My limbs trembled. A roaring in my ears, drowning out all other sounds. I dry-heaved and fell off Steve, almost tumbling into the river. "No!" I tried to scream. "Not now!" But I couldn't form the words. I was in the grip of immense pain and could do nothing against it.

Time seemed to collapse. Gripped by panic, I was dimly aware of Steve crawling on top of me. He wrestled my knife from my hand. There was a sharp stabbing sensation in my stomach, followed by another. Steve crowed, "Now I have you! Now you're gonna die!" Something blurry passed in front of my eyes, then back again. Fighting the white light inside my head, I got my eyes to focus. It was the knife. Steve had pulled it out and was waving it in my face, teasing me, sure he'd won, prolonging the moment of triumph.

But Steve had miscalculated. The pain of the stabbing brought me back from the brink of all-out confusion. The agony in my gut worked against the pain in my head, and the world began to swim back into place around me. Steve was perched on top of me, laughing. But I wasn't afraid. Unknown to himself, he was helping me. I was able to think halfway straight now, able to plan, able to act.

My right hand stole to the waistband of my pants as Steve continued to mock me. I gripped the handle of a second knife. I caught a glimpse of Mr. Tiny peering over Steve's shoulder. He'd seen my hand moving and knew what was coming. He was nodding, though I'm not sure if he was encouraging me or merely bobbing his head up and down with excitement.

I lay still, gathering my very last dredges of energy together, letting Steve torment me with wild promises of what was to come. I was bleeding freely from the stab wounds in my stomach. I wasn't sure if I'd be alive come the dawn, but of one thing I was certain — Steve would die before me.

"— and when I finish with your toes and fingers, I'll move on to your nose and ears!" Steve yelled. "But first I'll cut your eyelids off, so you can see everything that I'm gonna do. After that I'll —"

"Steve," I wheezed, stopping him midflow. "Want to know the secret of winning a fight like this? Less talking — more stabbing."

I lunged at him, using the muscles of my stomach to force my body up. Steve wasn't prepared for it. I knocked him backwards. As he fell, I swung my legs around, then pushed with my knees and feet, so I drove him all the way back with the full weight of my body. He hit the pavement with a grunt, for the second time within the space of a few minutes. This time he managed to hold on to his knife, but that was no use to him. I wasn't going to make the same mistake twice.

No hesitation. No pausing to pick my point. No cynical, memorable last words. I put my trust in the gods of the vampires and blindly thrust my knife forward. I brought it around and down in a savage arc, and by luck or fate drove it into the center of Steve's chest — clean through his shriveled forgery of a heart!

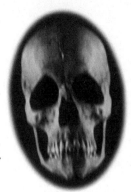

CHAPTER TWELVE

STEVE'S EYES AND MOUTH popped wide with shock. His expression was comical, but I was in no mood to laugh. There was no recovery from a strike like that. Steve was finished. But he could take me with him if I wasn't careful. So instead of celebrating, I grabbed his left hand, holding it down tight by his side so he couldn't use his knife on me.

Steve's gaze slid to the handle of the knife sticking out of his chest. "Oh," he said tonelessly. Then blood trickled from the sides of his mouth. His chest heaved up and down, the handle rising and falling with it. I wanted to pull the knife out, to end matters — he could maybe go on like this for a minute or two, the knife stopping the gush of blood from his heart — but my left hand was useless and I didn't dare free my right.

Then — applause. My head lifted, and Steve's eyes rolled back in their sockets so that he could look behind him. Mr. Tiny was clapping, bright red tears of joy dripping down his cheeks. "What passion!" he exclaimed. "What valor! What a never-say-die spirit! My money was always on you, Darren. It could have gone either way, but if I was a betting man, I'd have bet big on you. I said as much beforehand, didn't I, Evanna?"

"Yes, father," Evanna answered quietly. She was studying me sadly. Her lips moved silently, but even though she uttered no sounds, I was able to make out what she said. "To the victor, the spoils."

"Come, Darren," Mr. Tiny said. "Pull out the knife and tend to your wounds. They're not immediately life-threatening, but you should have a doctor see to them. Your friends in the stadium are almost done with their foes. They'll be coming soon. They can take you to a hospital."

I shook my head. I only meant that I couldn't pull the knife out, but Mr. Tiny must have thought I didn't want to kill Steve. "Don't be foolish," he snapped. "Steve is the enemy. He deserves no mercy. Finish him, then take your place as the rightful ruler of the night."

"You are the Lord of the Shadows now," Evanna said. "There is no room in your life for mercy. Do as my father bids. The sooner you accept your destiny, the easier it will be for you."

"And do you . . . want me to . . . kill Vancha now too?" I panted angrily.

"Not yet," Mr. Tiny laughed. "That will come in its own time." His laughter faded and his expression hardened. "Much will come in time. The vampaneze will fall, and so shall the humans. This world will be yours, Darren — rather, *ours*. Together we'll rule. Your hand at the tiller, my voice in your ear. I'll guide and advise you. Not openly — I don't have the power to directly steer you — but on the sly. I'll make suggestions, you'll heed them, and together we'll build a world of chaos and twisted beauty."

"What makes you . . . think I'd have anything to do . . . with a monster like you?" I snarled.

"He has a point, father," Evanna murmured. "We both know what lies in store for Darren. He will become a ruler of savage, unrelenting power. But he hates you. That hatred will increase over the centuries, not diminish. What makes you think you can rule with him?"

"I know more about the boy than you do," Mr. Tiny said smugly. "He will accept me. He was born to." Mr. Tiny squatted and looked straight down into

Steve's eyes. Then he looked up into mine, his face no more than two or three inches away. "I have always been there for you. For both of you," he whispered. "When you competed with your friends for a ticket to the Cirque Du Freak," he said to me, "I whispered in your ear and told you when to grab for it."

My jaw dropped. I *had* heard a voice that day, but I'd thought it was only an inner voice, the voice of instinct.

"And when you," he said to Steve, "noticed something strange about Darren after your meeting with Larten Crepsley, who do you think kept you awake at night, filling your thoughts with doubt and suspicion?"

Mr. Tiny pulled back a foot. His smile had returned, and it now threatened to spread from his face and fill the tunnel. "*I* influenced Crepsley and inspired him to blood Darren. *I* urged Gannen Harst to suggest Steve try the Coffin of Fire. Both of you have enjoyed enormous slices of good fortune in life. You put it down to the luck of the vampires, or the survival instinct of the vampaneze. But it was neither. You owe your nine cat's lives — and quite a few more — to *me*."

"I don't understand," I said, confused and alarmed. "Why would you go to all that trouble? Why ruin our lives?"

"*Ruin?*" he barked. "With my help you became a Prince and Steve became a Lord. With my backing the two of you have led the creatures of the night to war, and one of you — *you*, Darren! — now stands poised to become the most powerful tyrant in the history of the world. I have *made* your lives, not ruined them!"

"But why us?" I pressed. "We were ordinary kids. Why pick on Steve and me?"

"You were never ordinary," Mr. Tiny disagreed. "From birth — no, from conception you were both unique." He stood and looked at Evanna. She was staring at him uncertainly — this was news to her too. "For a long time I wondered what it would be like to father children," Mr. Tiny said softly. "When, spurred on by a stubborn vampire, I finally decided to give parenthood a try, I created two offspring in my own mold, beings of magic and great power.

"Evanna and Hibernius fascinated me at first, but in time I grew tired of their limitations. Because they can see into the future, they — like me — are limited in what they can do in the present. All of us have to abide by laws not of our making. I can interfere in the affairs of mankind more than my children can, but not as much as I'd wish. In many ways my hands are tied. I can influence mortals, and I do, but they're contrary creatures and short-lived. It's difficult to manipulate large groups of humans over a long period of time — especially now that there are billions of them!

"What I longed for was a mortal I could channel my will through, a being not bound by the laws of the universe, nor shackled by the confines of humanity. My ally would have to start as a human, then become a vampire or vampaneze. With my help he would lead his clan to rule over all. Together we could govern the course of the world for hundreds of years to come, and through *his* children I could control it for thousands of years — maybe even the rest of time itself."

"You're insane," I growled. "I don't care if you did help me. I won't work with you or do what you want. I'm not going to link myself to your warped cause. I doubt that Steve would have either, if he'd won."

"But you *will* join me," Mr. Tiny insisted, "just as Steve would have. You must. It's in your nature. Like sides with like." He paused, then said proudly and provocatively, "Son sides with father."

"*What?*" Evanna exploded, leaping to an understanding sooner than I did.

"I required a less powerful heir," Mr. Tiny said, his gaze fixed on me. "One who'd carry my genes and mirror my desires, but who could act freely as a mortal. To weed out any weaknesses, I created a pair, then set them against each other. The weaker would perish and be forgotten. The stronger would go on to claim the world." He stuck his arms out, the gesture both mocking and strangely heartfelt. "Come and give your father a hug, Darren — *my son!*"

CHAPTER THIRTEEN

"YOU'RE INSANE!" I CROAKED. "I have a father, a real dad. It isn't you!"

"Dermot Shan was not your father," Mr. Tiny replied. "You were a cuckoo's child. Steve too. I did my work quietly, unknown to your mothers. But trust me — you're both mine."

"This is outrageous!" Evanna screeched, her body expanding, becoming more that of a wolf than human, until she filled most of the tunnel. "It is forbidden! How dare you!"

"I acted within the confines of the universe's laws!" Mr. Tiny snapped. "You'd know if I had not — all would be chaos. I stretched them a bit, but I didn't break them. I am allowed to breed, and my children — if they lack my magical powers — can act the same way as any normal mortal."

"But if Darren and Steve are your sons, then *you* have created the future where one of them becomes the Lord of the Shadows!" Evanna roared. "*You* have cast mankind into the abyss, and twisted the strands of the future to suit your own foul needs!"

"Yes," Mr. Tiny chuckled, then pointed a finger at Evanna. "Do not cross me on this, daughter. I would not harm my own flesh and blood, but I could make life very unpleasant if you got on the wrong side of me."

Evanna glared at her father hatefully, then gradually resumed her regular shape and size. "This is unjust," she muttered. "The universe will punish you, perhaps not immediately, but eventually you'll pay a price for your arrogance."

"I doubt it," Mr. Tiny smirked. "Mankind was heading toward an all-time boring low. Peace, prosperity, global communication, brotherly love — where's the fun in *that*? Yes, there were still plenty of wars and conflicts to enjoy, but I could see the people of the world moving ever closer together. I did my best, nudged nations along the path to battle, sowed seeds of discontent everywhere I could, even helped get a few tyrants wrongfully elected to some of the most powerful positions on Earth — I was sure those fine specimens would push the world to the brink!

"But no! No matter how tense things got, no matter

how much meddling my minions did, I could see peace and understanding gradually winning through. It was time for drastic action, to take the world back to the good old days, when everyone was at everybody else's throat. I've simply restored the natural order of beautiful chaos. The universe won't punish me for that. If anything, I expect —"

"Shut up!" I screamed, surprising both Mr. Tiny and Evanna. "It's bull, all of it! You're not my father! You're a monster!"

"And so are you," Mr. Tiny beamed. "Or soon will be. But don't worry, son — monsters have all the fun!"

I stared at him, sickened, senses reeling, unable to take it all in. If this was true, everything in my life had been false. I was never the person I thought I was, only a pawn of Mr. Tiny's, a time bomb waiting to explode. I'd been blooded simply to extend my life, so I could live longer and do more of Mr. Tiny's work. My war with Steve had served only to get rid of the weaker of us, so that the stronger could emerge as a more powerful beast. I'd done nothing for the sake of the vampires or my family and friends — everything had been for Mr. Tiny. And now that I'd proved myself worthy, I'd become a dictator and lay low anyone who opposed him. My wishes would count for nothing. It was my destiny.

"Fa-fa-fa . . ." Steve stammered, spitting blood from his mouth. With his free hand he reached out to Mr. Tiny. "Father," he managed to croak. "Help . . . me."

"Why?" Mr. Tiny sniffed.

"I . . . never . . . had . . . a . . . Dad." Each word was a heart-churning effort, but Steve forced them out. "I . . . want . . . to . . . know . . . you. I'll . . . serve . . . you . . . and . . . love . . . you."

"What on earth would I want with *love*?" Mr. Tiny laughed. "Love is one of the most basic human emotions. I'm so pleased I was never cursed with it. Servitude, gratitude, fear, hatred, anger — these I like. Love . . . you can take your love to the Lake of Souls when you die. Perhaps it will provide you with some comfort there."

"But . . . I'm . . . your . . . son," Steve cried weakly.

"You were," Mr. Tiny sneered. "Now you're just a loser, and soon you'll be dead meat. I'll toss your carcass to my Little People to eat — that's how little I feel for you. This is a winner's world. Second place equals second rate. You're nothing to me. Darren's my only son now."

The pain in Steve's eyes was awful to behold. As a child, he'd been crushed when he thought I'd betrayed him. Now he'd been openly mocked and disowned by his father. It destroyed him. His heart had been full of hatred before this, but now that it was down to its last few beats, there was room only for despair.

But in Steve's anguish I found hope. Consumed by smugness, Mr. Tiny had revealed too much, too soon. At the back of my brain an idea sparked into life. In a whirl I began to put various pieces together — Mr. Tiny's revelation and Evanna's reaction. Evanna said Mr. Tiny had created the future in which Steve or I was the Lord of the Shadows. He'd bent the laws he and she lived by, to twist things around and build a chaotic world that he and I could rule over. Evanna and Mr. Tall had told me there was no escaping the Lord of the Shadows, that he was part of the world's future. But they were wrong. He was part of *Mr. Tiny's* future. Des Tiny might be the most powerful individual in the universe, but he was still only an individual. What one individual could build, another could destroy.

Mr. Tiny's eyes were on Steve. He was laughing at him, enjoying Steve's dying misery. Evanna's head was bowed — she'd given in and accepted this. Not me. If I'd inherited Mr. Tiny's evil, destructive streak, I'd also inherited his cunning. I'd stop at nothing to deny him his vision of a ruined future.

Slowly, ever so slowly, I released Steve's left hand and moved my arm away. He had a free shot at my stomach now, in the perfect position to finish the job he'd started when he stabbed me earlier. But Steve didn't notice. He was wrapped up in his sorrow. I faked a cough and plucked at his left sleeve. If Mr. Tiny had seen it, he could have stopped my plan there. But he thought he'd won, that it was all over. He couldn't even imagine the vaguest possibility of a threat.

Steve's gaze flickered down. He realized his hand was free. He saw his chance to kill me. His fingers stiffened on the handle of his knife . . . then relaxed. For a terrible moment I thought he'd died, but then I saw that he was still alive. What made him pause was doubt. He'd spent most of his life hating me, but now he'd been told I was his brother. I could see his brain churning. I was a victim of Des Tiny, just as he was. He'd been wrong to hate me — I'd had no choice in what I'd done. In all the world, I was the person he should be closest to, and instead I was the person he'd hurt the most.

What Steve found in those last few moments was what I thought he'd lost forever — his humanity. He saw the error of his ways, the evil he'd committed, the mistakes he'd made. There was possible salvation in that recognition. Now that he could see himself for what he truly was, perhaps, even at this late stage, he could repent.

But I couldn't afford humanity. Steve's salvation would be my undoing — and the world's. I needed him mad as hell, fire in his gut, filled with fury and hate. Only in that state could he find the power to maybe help me break Des Tiny's hold over the future.

"Steve," I said, forcing a wicked smile. "You were right. I *did* plot with Mr. Crepsley to take your place as his assistant. We made a fool of you, and I'm glad. You're a nobody. A nothing. This is what you deserve. If Mr. Crepsley were alive, he'd be laughing at you now, just like the rest of us are."

Mr. Tiny howled with delight. "That's my boy!" he hooted. He thought I was getting one last dig in before Steve died. But he was wrong.

Steve's eyes refilled with hatred. The human within him vanished in an instant and he was Steve Leopard, vampire killer, again. In one fast, crazed movement he brought his left hand up and drove his knife deep into my stomach. Less than a second later he did it again, then again.

"Stop!" Mr. Tiny yelled, seeing the danger too late. He lurched at us, to pull me off, but Evanna slid in front of him and blocked his way.

"No, father!" she snapped. "You cannot interfere in this!"

"Get out of my way!" he bellowed, struggling with

her. "The fool's going to let Leonard kill him! We have to stop it!"

"Too late," I giggled, as Steve's blade slid in and sliced through my guts for a fifth time. Mr. Tiny stopped and blinked dumbly, at a complete loss for what may well have been the first time in his long, ungodly life. "Destiny . . . rejected," I said with my final whole breath. Then I grabbed Steve tight as he lunged at me with his knife again, and rolled to my right, off the edge of the path, into the river.

We went into the water together, wrapped in each other's arms, and sank quickly. Steve tried stabbing me again, but it was too much for him. He went limp and fell away from me, his dead body dropping into the dark depths of the river, disappearing from sight within sounds.

I was barely conscious, hanging sluggishly, limbs being picked at and made to sway by the current of the river. Water rushed down my throat and flooded my lungs. Part of me wanted to strike for the surface, but I fought against it, not wanting to give Mr. Tiny even the slightest opportunity to revive me.

I saw faces in the water, or in my thoughts — impossible to tell the difference. Sam Grest, Gavner Purl, Arra Sails, Mr. Tall, Shancus, R.V., Mr. Crepsley. The dead, come to welcome me.

I stretched my arms out to them, but our fingers didn't touch. I imagined Mr. Crepsley waving, and a sad expression crossed his face. Then everything faded. I stopped struggling. The world, the water, the faces faded from sight, then from memory. A roaring that was silence. A darkness that was light. A chill that burnt. One final flutter of my eyelids, barely a movement, impossibly tiring. And then, in the lonely, watery darkness of the river, as all must do when the Grim Reaper calls — I died.

INTERLUDE

TIMELESSNESS. ETERNAL GLOOM. DRIFTING in slow, never-ending circles. Surrounded but alone. Aware of other souls, trapped like me, but unable to contact them. No sense of sight, hearing, taste, smell, touch. Only the crushing boredom of the present and painful memories of the past.

I know this place. It's the Lake of Souls, a zone where spirits go when they can't leave Earth's pull. Some people's souls don't move on when they die. They remain trapped in the waters of this putrid lake, condemned to swirl silently in the depths for all eternity.

I'm sad I ended up here, but not surprised. I tried to live a good life, and I sacrificed myself at the end in an effort to save others, so in those respects I was maybe deserving of Paradise. But I was also a killer. Whatever my reasons, I took lives and created unhappiness. I don't know if some higher power has passed judgment on me, or if I'm imprisoned by my own guilt. It doesn't really matter, I guess. I'm here and there's no getting out. This is my lot. Forever.

No sense of time. No days, nights, hours, minutes — not even seconds. Have I been here a week, a year, a century? Can't tell. Does the War of the Scars still rage? Have the vampires or vampaneze fallen? Has another taken my place as the Lord of the Shadows? Did I die for no reason? I don't know. I probably never will. That's part of my sentence. Part of my curse.

If the souls of the dead could speak, they'd scream for release. Not just release from the Lake, but from their memories. Memories gnaw away at me relentlessly. I remember so much of my past, all the times where I failed or could have done better. With nothing else to do, I'm forced to review my life, over and over. Even my most minor errors become supreme lapses of judgment. They torment me worse than Steve ever did.

I try to hide from the pain of the memories by retreating further into my past. I remember the young Darren Shan, human, happy, normal, innocent. I spend years, decades — or is it just minutes? — reliving the simple, carefree times. I piece together my entire early life. I recall even the smallest details — the colors of toy cars, homework assignments, throwaway conversations. I go through everyday chat a hundred times, until every word is correct. The longer I think about it, the deeper into those years I sink, losing myself, human again, almost able to believe that the memories are reality, and my death and the Lake of Souls nothing but an unpleasant dream.

But eternity can't be dodged forever. My later memories are always hovering, picking away at the boundaries of the limited reality that I've built. Every so often I flash ahead to a face or event. Then I lose control and find myself thrust into the darker, nightmarish world of my life as a half-vampire. I relive the mistakes, the wrong choices, the bloodshed.

So many friends lost, so many enemies killed. I feel

responsible for all of them. I believed in peace when I first went to Vampire Mountain. Even though Kurda Smahlt betrayed his people, I felt sorry for him. I knew he did it in an effort to avoid war. I couldn't under-stand why it had come to this. If only the vampires and vampaneze had sat down and talked through their dif-ferences, war could have been avoided.

When I first became a Prince, I dreamed of being a peacemaker, taking up where Kurda left off, bringing the vampaneze back into the clan. I lost those dreams somewhere during the six years I spent living within Vampire Mountain. Surviving as a vampire, learning their ways, training with weapons, sending friends out to fight and die . . . It all rubbed off on me, and when I finally returned to the world beyond the mountain, I'd changed. I was a warrior, fierce, unmoved by death, intent on killing rather than talking.

I wasn't evil. Sometimes it's necessary to fight. There are occasions when you have to cast aside your nobler ideals and get your hands dirty. But you should always strive for peace, and search to find the peaceful solution to even the most bloody of conflicts. I didn't do that. I embraced the war and went along with the general opinion — that if we killed the Vampaneze Lord, all our problems would be solved and life would be hunky-dory.

We were wrong. The death of one man never solved anything. Steve was just the start. Once you set off down the road of murder, it's hard to take a detour. We couldn't have stopped. The death of one foe wouldn't have been enough. We'd have set about annihilating the vampaneze after Steve, then humanity. We'd have established ourselves as the rulers of the world, crushing all in our path, and I'd have gone along with it. No, more than that — I'd have led, not just followed.

That guilt, not just of what I've done but of what I would have done, eats away at me like a million ravenous rats. It doesn't matter that I'm the son of Desmond Tiny, that wickedness was in my genes. I had the power to break away from the dark designs of my father. I proved that at the end, by letting myself die. But why didn't I do it sooner, before so many people were killed?

I don't know if I could have stopped the war, but I could have said, "No, I don't want any part of this." I could have argued for peace, not fought for it. If I'd failed, at least I maybe wouldn't have wound up here, weighed down by the chains of so many grisly deaths.

Time passes. Faces swim in and out of my thoughts. Memories form, are forgotten, form again. I blank out large parts of my life, recover them, blank them out again. I succumb to madness and forget who I was. But the madness doesn't last. I reluctantly return to my senses.

I think about my friends a lot, especially those who were alive when I died. Did any of them perish in the stadium? If they survived that, what came next? Since Steve and I both died, what happened with the War of the Scars? Could Mr. Tiny replace us with new leaders, men with the same powers as Steve and me? Hard to see how, unless he fathered another couple of children.

Was Harkat alive now, pushing for peace between the vampires and vampaneze, like he had when he was Kurda Smahlt? Had Alice Burgess led her vampirites against the vampets and crushed them? Did Debbie mourn for me? Not knowing was an agony. I'd have sold my soul to the Devil for a few minutes in the world of the living, where I could find answers to my questions. But not even the Devil disturbed the waters of the Lake of Souls. This was the exclusive resting place of the dead and the damned.

Drifting, ghostly, resigned. I fixate on my death, remembering Steve's face as he stabbed me, his hatred, his fear. I count the number of seconds it took me to die, the drops of blood I spilled on the riverbank where he killed me. I feel myself topple into the water of the river a dozen times . . . a hundred . . . a thousand.

That water was so much more alive than the water of the Lake of Souls. Currents. Fish swam in it. Air bubbles. Cold. The water here is dead, as lifeless as the souls it contains. No fish explore its depths, no insects skim its surface. I'm not sure how I'm aware of these facts, but I am. I sense the awful emptiness of the Lake. It exists solely to hold the spirits of the miserable dead.

I long for the river. I'd meet any asking price if I could go back and experience the rush of flowing water again, the chill as I fell in, the pain as I bled to death. Anything's better than this limbo world. Even a minute of dying is preferable to an eternity of nothingness.

One small measure of comfort — as bad as this is for me, it must be much worse for Steve. My guilt is nothing compared to his. I was sucked into Mr. Tiny's evil games, but Steve threw himself heart and soul into them. His crimes far outweigh mine, so his suffering must be that much more.

Unless he doesn't accept his guilt. Perhaps eternity

means nothing to him. Maybe he's just mad that I beat him. It could be that he doesn't worry about what he did, or realize just how much of a monster he was. He might be content here, reflecting with fondness on all that he achieved.

But I doubt it. I suspect Mr. Tiny's admission destroyed a large part of Steve's mad defenses. Knowing that he was my brother, and that we were both puppets in our father's hands, must have shaken him up. I think, given the time to reflect — and that's all one can do here — he'll weep for what he did. He'll see himself for what he truly was, and hate himself for it.

I shouldn't take pleasure in that. There, but for the grace of the gods . . . But I still despise Steve. I can understand why he acted that way, and I'm sorry for him. But I can't forgive him. I can't stretch that far. Perhaps that's another reason why I'm here.

I'm retreating from the painful memories again. Withdrawing from the vampire world, pretending it never happened. I imagine myself as a child, living the same days over and over, refusing to go beyond the afternoon when I won a ticket to the Cirque Du Freak. I build a perfect, sealed-off, comfortable reality. I'm Darren

Shan, loving son and brother, not the best-behaved boy in the world, but far from the worst. I do chores for Mom and Dad, struggle with homework, watch TV, hang out with my friends. One moment I'm six or seven years old, the next ten or eleven. Continually twisting back upon myself, living the past, ignoring all that I don't want to think about. Steve's my best friend. We read comics, watch horror movies, tell jokes to each other. Annie's a child, always a child — I never think of her as a woman with a son of her own. Vampires are monsters of myth, like werewolves, zombies, mummies, not to be taken seriously.

It's my aim to become the Darren of my memories, to lose myself completely in the past. I don't want to deal with the guilt anymore. I've gone mad before and recovered. I want to go mad again, but this time let madness swallow me whole.

I struggle to vanish into the past. Remembering everything, painting the details more precisely every time I revisit a moment. I start to forget about the souls, the Lake, the vampires and vampaneze. I still get occasional flashes of reality, but I clamp down on them quickly. Thinking as a child, remembering as a child, becoming a child.

I'm almost there. The madness waits, arms spread wide, welcoming me. I'll be living a lie, but it will be a peaceful, soothing lie. I long for it. I work hard to make it real. And I'm getting there. I feel myself sliding closer toward it. I reach for the lie with the tendrils of my mind. I feel around it, explore it, start to slip inside it, when all of a sudden — a new sensation . . .

Pain! Heaviness. Rising. The madness is left behind. The water of the Lake closes around me. Searing pain! Thrashing, coughing, gasping. *But with what?* I have no arms to thrash, no mouth to cough, no lungs to gasp. Is this part of the madness? Am I . . .

And suddenly my head — an actual, real *head*! — breaks the surface. I'm breathing air. Sunlight blinds me. I spit water out. My arms come clear of the Lake. I'm surrounded, but not by the souls of the dead — by nets! People pulling on them. Coming out of the Lake. Screaming with pain and confusion — but no sounds. Body forming, incredibly heavy after all this weightless time. I land on hard, warm earth. My feet drag out of the water. Amazed, I try to stand. I make it to my knees, then fall. I hit the ground hard. Pain again, fresh and frightening. I curl up into a ball, shivering like a baby. I shut my eyes against the light and dig my fingers into the earth to reassure myself that it's real. And then I sob feebly as the incredible, bewildering, impossible realization sinks in — *I'm alive*!

PART TWO

CHAPTER FOURTEEN

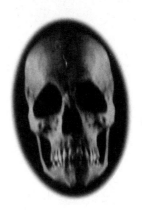

THE SUN HAMMERED DOWN fiercely upon me, but I couldn't stop shivering. Someone threw a blanket around me, hairy and thick. It itched like mad, but the sensation was delicious. Any sensation would have been welcome after the numbness of the Lake of Souls.

The person who'd draped the blanket over me knelt by my side and tilted my head back. I blinked water from my eyes and focused. It took a few seconds, but finally I fixed on my rescuer. It was a Little Person. At first I thought it was Harkat. I opened my mouth to shout his name happily. Then I did a double take and realized this wasn't my old friend, just one of his grey, scarred, green-eyed kind.

The Little Person examined me silently, prodding and poking. Then he stood and stepped aside, leaving me. I wrapped the blanket tighter around myself, trying to stop the shivers. After a while I worked up the strength to look around. I was lying by the rim of the Lake of Souls. The earth around me was hard and dry, like desert. Several Little People stood nearby. A couple were hanging up nets to dry — the nets they'd fished me out with. The others simply stared off into space or at the Lake.

There was a screeching sound high overhead. Looking up, I saw a huge winged beast circling the Lake. From my previous trip here, I knew it was a dragon. My insides clenched with fear. Then I noticed a second dragon. A third. A fourth. Jaw dropping, I realized the sky was full of them, dozens, maybe hundreds. If they caught sight of me . . .

I started to scramble weakly for safety, then paused and glanced at the Little People. They knew the dragons were there, but they weren't bothered by the giant flying reptiles. They might have dragged me out of the Lake to feed me to the dragons, but I didn't think so. And even if they had, in my feeble state I could do nothing about it. I couldn't flee or fight, and there was nowhere to hide. So I just lay where I was and waited for events to run their course.

For several minutes the dragons circled and the Little People stood motionless. I was still filled with a great chill, but I wasn't shivering quite as much as when I first came out of the Lake. I was gathering what small amounts of energy I could call on, to try and walk over to the Little People and quiz them about what was going on, when somebody spoke behind me.

"Sorry I'm late."

I looked over my shoulder, expecting Mr. Tiny, but it was his daughter, (my half-sister!) Evanna, striding toward me. She looked no different from how I remembered her, though there was a sparkle in her green and brown eyes that had been absent when last we met.

"Whuh!" I croaked, the only sound I was able to make.

"Easy," Evanna said, reaching me and bending to squeeze my shoulder warmly. "Don't try to speak. It will take a few hours for the effects of the Lake to wear off. I'll build a fire and cook some broth for you. That's why I wasn't here when you were fished out — I was looking for firewood." She pointed to a mound of logs and branches.

I wanted to besiege her with questions, but there was no point taxing my throat when it wasn't ready to work. So I said nothing as she picked me up and carried me to the pile of wood like a baby, then set me down and turned her attention to the kindling.

When the fire was burning nicely, Evanna took a flat circular object out from beneath the ropes she was wearing. I recognized it immediately — a collapsible pot, the same sort that Mr. Crepsley had once used. She pressed it in the middle, causing it to pop outward and assume its natural shape, then filled it with water (not from the Lake, but from a bucket) and some grass and herbs, and hung it from a stick over the flames.

The broth was weak and tasteless, but its warmth was like the fire of the gods to me. I drank deeply, one bowl, another, a third. Evanna smiled as I slurped, then sipped slowly from a bowl of her own. The dragons screeched at regular intervals overhead, the sun burned brightly, and the scent of the smoke was magical. I felt strangely relaxed, as if this was a lazy summer Sunday afternoon.

I was halfway through my fourth bowl before my stomach growled at me to say, "Enough!" Sighing happily, I laid the bowl down and sat, smiling lightly, thinking only of the good feelings inside. But I couldn't sit silently forever, so eventually I raised my gaze, looked at Evanna, and tested my vocal chords. "Urch," I creaked — I'd meant to say "Thanks."

"It's been a long time since you spoke," Evanna said. "Start simply. Try the alphabet. I will hunt for more wood, to sustain the fire. We won't be staying here much longer, but we may as well have warmth while we are. Practice while I am gone, and we can maybe talk when I return."

I did as the witch advised. At first I struggled to produce sounds anything like they should be, but I stuck with it and gradually my As started to sound like As, my Bs like Bs, and so on. When I'd run through the alphabet several times without making a mistake, I moved on to words, simple stuff to begin with — cat, dog, Mom, Dad, sky, me. I tried names after that, longer words, and finally sentences. It hurt to speak, and I slurred some words, but when Evanna eventually came back, clutching an armful of pitiful twigs, I was able to greet her in a gravelly but semi-normal voice. "Thanks for the broth."

"You're welcome." She threw some of the twigs onto the fire, then sat beside me. "How do you feel?"

"Rough as rust."

"Do you remember your name?"

I squinted at her oddly. "Why shouldn't I?"

"The Lake twists the minds of people," she said. "It can destroy memories. Many of the souls forget who they are. They go mad and lose track of their pasts. You were in there a long time. I feared the worst."

"I came close," I admitted, hunching up closer to the fire, recalling my attempts to go mad and escape the weight of my memories. "It was horrible. Easier to be crazy in there than sane."

"So what is it?" Evanna asked. When I blinked dumbly, she laughed. "Your name?"

"Oh." I smiled. "Darren. Darren Shan. I'm a half-vampire. I remember it all, the War of the Scars, Mr. Crepsley, Steve." My features darkened. "I remember my death, and what Mr. Tiny said just before it."

"Quite the one for surprises, isn't he — our father?"

She looked at me sideways to see what I'd say about that, but I couldn't think of anything — how do you respond to the news that Des Tiny is your dad, and a centuries-old witch is your half-sister? To avoid the subject, I studied the land around me. "This place looks different," I said. "It was green when I came with Harkat, lots of grass and fresh earth."

"This is further into the future," Evanna explained. "Before, you traveled a mere two hundred or so years ahead of the present. This time you have come hundreds of thousands of years, maybe more. I'm not entirely certain. This is the first time our father has ever allowed me to come here."

"Hundreds of . . ." My head spun.

"This is the age of dragons," Evanna said. "The age after mankind."

My breath caught in my throat, and I had to clear

it twice before I could respond. "You mean humanity has died out?"

"Died out or moved on to other worlds or spheres." Evanna shrugged. "I cannot say for sure. I know only that the world belongs to dragons now. They control it as humans once did, and dinosaurs before them."

"And the War of the Scars?" I asked nervously. "Who won that?"

Evanna was silent a moment. Then she said, "We have much to speak about. Let's not rush." She pointed at the dragons high above us. "Call one of them down."

"What?" I frowned.

"Call them, the way you used to call Madam Octa. You can control dragons like you controlled your pet spider."

"How?" I asked, bewildered.

"I will show you. But first — call." She smiled. "They will not harm us. You have my word."

I wasn't too sure about that, but how cool would it be to control a dragon! Looking up, I studied the creatures in the sky, then fixed on one slightly smaller than the others. (I didn't want to bring a large one down, in case Evanna was wrong and it attacked.) I tracked it with my eyes for a few seconds, then stretched out a hand toward it and whispered, "Come to me. Come down. Come, my beauty."

The dragon executed a backward somersault, then dropped swiftly. I thought it was going to blast us into a thousand pieces. I panicked and tried to run. Evanna hauled me back into place. "Calmly," she said. "You cannot control it if you break contact, and now that it knows we are here, it would be dangerous to let it have its own way."

I didn't want to play this game, but it was too late to back out now. With my heart beating fiercely, I fixed on the swooping dragon and spoke to it again. "Easy. Pull up. I don't want to hurt you — and I don't want you to hurt us! Just hover above us a bit and . . ."

The dragon pulled out of its fall and came to a halt several yards overhead. It flapped its leathery wings powerfully. I could hear nothing over the sound, and the force of the air knocked me backward. As I struggled to right myself, the dragon came to land close beside me. It tucked its wings in, thrust its head down as though it meant to gobble me up, then stopped and just stared.

The beast was much like those I'd seen before. Its wings were a light green color, it was about twenty feet long, scaled like a snake, with a bulging chest and thin tail. The scales on its stomach were a dull red and gold color, while those on top were green with red flecks. It had two long forelegs near the front of its body, and two small hind legs about a quarter of the way from the rear. Lots of sharp claws. A head like an alligator, long and flat, with bulging yellow eyes and small pointed ears. Its face was dark purple. It also had a long forked tongue and, if it was like the other dragons, it could blow fire.

"It's incredible," Evanna said. "This is the first time I have seen one up so close. Our father outdid himself with this creation."

"Mr. Tiny made the dragons?"

Evanna nodded. "He helped human scientists create them. Actually, one of your friends was a key member of the team — Alan Morris. With our father's aid he made a breakthrough that allowed them to be cloned from a combination of dinosaur cells."

"*Alan?*" I snorted. "You're telling me Alan Morris made dragons? That's total and utter . . ." I stopped short. Tommy had told me Alan was a scientist, and that he'd specialized in cloning. It was hard to believe the foolish boy I'd known had grown up to become a creator of dinosaurs — but then again, it was hard to believe Steve had become the Vampaneze Lord, or myself a Vampire Prince. I suppose all influential men and women must start out as normal, unremarkable children.

"For many centuries, the rulers of this world will

keep the dragons in check," Evanna said. "They'll control them. Later, when they lose their hold on power — as all rulers must — the dragons will fly free and multiply, becoming a real menace. In the end they'll outlive or outlast all the humans, vampires and vampaneze, and rule the world in their turn. I'm not sure what comes after them. I've never looked that far ahead."

"Why doesn't it kill us?" I asked, eyeing the dragon uneasily. "Is it tame?"

"Hardly!" Evanna laughed. "Normally the dragons would tear us apart. Our father masks this area from them — they can't see the Lake of Souls or anyone around it."

"This one sees us," I noted.

"Yes, but you're controlling it, so we are safe."

"The last time I was here, I was almost roasted alive by dragons," I said. "How can I control them now when I couldn't before?"

"But you could," Evanna replied. "You had the power — you just didn't know it. The dragons would have obeyed you then, as they do now."

"Why?" I frowned. "What's so special about me?"

"You're Desmond Tiny's son," Evanna reminded me. "Even though he did not pass on his magical powers to you, traces of his influence remain. That is why you were skilled at controlling animals such as spiders and wolves. But there is more to it than that."

Evanna reached out, her hand extending far beyond its natural length, and touched the dragon's head. Its skull glowed beneath the witch's touch. Its purple skin faded, then became translucent, so I could see inside to its brain. The oval, stone-like shape was instantly familiar, though it took me a few seconds to recall what it reminded me of. Then it clicked.

"The Stone of Blood!" I exclaimed. While this was much smaller than the one in the Hall of Princes, it was unmistakably the same type. The Stone of Blood had been a gift to the vampires from Mr. Tiny. For seven hundred years the members of the clan had fed their blood to it, and used it to keep track of and communicate with each other. It was an invaluable tool, but dangerous — if it had fallen into the hands of the vampaneze, they could have tracked down and killed almost every living vampire.

"Our father took the brain of a dragon into the past and gave it to the vampires," Evanna said. "He often does that — travels into the past and makes small changes that influence the present and future. Through the Stone of Blood he bound the vampires more tightly to his will. If the vampires win the War of

the Scars, they will use the Stone to control the dragons, and through them the skies. I don't think the vampaneze will use it if they win. They never trusted this
gift of Desmond Tiny's — it was one of the reasons
they broke away from the rest of the vampire clan. I'm
not sure what their relationship with the dragons
would be like. Perhaps our father will provide them
with some other way of controlling the beasts — or
maybe it will please him to let them be enemies."

"The Stone of Blood was supposed to be the clan's
last hope," I muttered, unable to take my eyes off the
dragon's glowing brain. "There was a legend — if we
lost the war with the vampaneze, the Stone of Blood
might some night help us rise again."

Evanna nodded and removed her hand from the
dragon's head. It stopped glowing and resumed its
normal appearance. The dragon didn't seem to have
noticed any change. It continued staring at me, await-
ing my command.

"Above all else, our father craves chaos," Evanna
said. "Stability bores him. He has no interest in seeing
any race rule forever. For a time it pleased him to let
humans rule this planet, since they were violent, always
at war with one another. But when he saw them heading the way of peace during the latter half of the twentieth century — or thought he did; to be honest, I don't

agree with his assessment — he set about overthrowing them. He will do the same with their successors.

"If the vampaneze win the War of the Scars and wipe out the vampires, he'll use the Stone in the future. He will lead humans to it and teach them to extract the blood cells and build a new army of cloned vampires. But they won't be vampires as you know them. Desmond will control the cloning process and meddle with the cells, twisting and reshaping them. The new creatures will be more savage than the original vampires, with less-developed brains, slaves to the whim of our father." Evanna smiled twistedly. "So yes, our father told the truth when he said the Stone of Blood could help the vampires rise again — but he kept a few of the less savory facts to himself."

"Then neither side can truly win," I said. "He's just setting the victors up for a later fall."

"That has always been Desmond's way," Evanna said. "What he helps create, he later destroys. Many empires — Egyptian, Persian, British — have already learned that to their cost."

"Egyptian?" I blinked.

"Our father is a great fan of empires," Evanna said. "Cavemen hitting each other with sticks and bones were of very limited interest to him. He prefers to see people killing each other with more effective weapons, and in greater numbers. But for mankind to advance barbarically, it also had to advance in other ways. It had to grow socially, culturally, spiritually, technologically, medically. Only a nation that was great in all aspects could wage war greatly.

"Our father has had his hand in most of the notable architectural, technical, or medical breakthroughs of mankind. He could never openly lead, but he influenced slyly. The only area where he had no real power was that of literature. Desmond is not a fictional dreamer. Reality is everything to him. He has no interest in the wonderful stories of mankind. Writers have always been alien to him — he does not read works of fiction, or take any notice of them."

"Never mind that," I grunted, not giving a hoot about Mr. Tiny's choice of reading material. "Tell me more about his meddling with mankind, and time-traveling. You say Mr. Tiny goes into the past to change the present and future. But what about the time paradox?" I'd seen lots of science fiction movies and TV shows. I knew all about the problems associated with the theory of time travel.

"There is no paradox," Evanna said. "The universe keeps natural order. The key events of the past cannot be changed — only the people involved."

"Huh?" I said.

"Once something important happens in the present — the universe, to give the higher force a name, decides what is important or not — it can never be changed," Evanna explained. "But you can alter the people involved. For instance, now that it has happened, you cannot travel to the past and prevent World War Two — but you *could* go back and kill Adolf Hitler. The universe would immediately create another person to fill his shoes. That person would be born like any normal person, grow up, then do what Hitler did, with precisely the same results. The name would change, but nothing else."

"But Hitler was a monster," I said. "He murdered millions of people. Do you mean, if Mr. Tiny went back and killed him, some innocent guy would take his place? All those people would still die?"

"Yes," Evanna said.

"But then that person wouldn't have chosen their fate," I frowned. "They wouldn't be responsible for their actions."

Evanna sniffed. "The universe would have to create a child with the potential for wickedness — a good man cannot be forced to do evil — but once it did, yes, that person would become a victim of destiny. It does not happen often. Our father only occasionally replaces important figures of the past. Most people have free will. But there *are* a few who don't."

"Am I one of them?" I asked quietly, fearing the answer.

"Most definitely not," Evanna smiled. "Your time is the present time, and you are an original creation. Though you were manipulated by our father since birth, the path you trod had not been laid down by anyone before you."

Evanna thought for a few seconds, then tried to explain the situation in a way that I could more easily understand.

"Although our father cannot change the events of the past, he can make minor alterations," she said. "If something happens in the present that is not to his liking, he can return to the past and create a train of events designed to lead to a solution to whatever is troubling him. That's how vampires came to be so numerous and powerful."

"Mr. Tiny created vampires?" I shouted — there was a myth that he'd made us, but I'd never believed it.

"No," Evanna said. "Vampires came into being by themselves. But there were never many of them. They were weak and disorganized. Then, in the middle of the twentieth century, our father decided mankind was taking a path toward peace and unity. Disliking it, he traveled to the past and spent a couple of decades trying different approaches to undermine humanity. In the end he settled on vampires. He gave them extra strength and speed, the power to flit and share their thoughts — all the supernatural abilities you know about. He also provided them with leaders who would knock them into shape and turn them into an army.

"As powerful as the clan became, our father ensured that they couldn't be a threat to humans. Originally vampires were able to come out by day — Desmond Tiny made them prisoners of the night, and robbed them of the gift of childbirth. Carefully shackled and maintained this way, the vampires had to live separately to the world of man and remain in the shadows. Since they didn't change anything important in the human history, the universe let them exist, and they eventually become part of the present — which is when our father was free to use them however he wished."

"And the present was my time?" I asked.

"Yes," Evanna said. "Time passes at the same rate, whether our father is in the past, present, or future. So, since he spent almost twenty years stuck in the past, trying to find a way to topple humanity, it was late in the twentieth century when he returned to the present."

"And because vampires were now part of that

present," I said, my brain hurting as I tried to keep up with all this mind-boggling information, "they were free to influence the future?"

"Correct," Evanna said. "But our father then saw that the clan wouldn't launch an attack on humanity if left to their own devices — they were content to stay out of the affairs of men. So he went back again — just for a few months this time — and engineered the vampaneze breakaway. By then planting the legend of the Lord of the Vampaneze, he edged them toward conflict with the vampires."

"And that led to the War of the Scars, and eventually the downfall of humanity," I growled, sick at the thought of the little man's terrible slyness.

"Well," Evanna smiled, "that was the plan."

"Do you mean —" I began to say excitedly, sensing hope in her smile.

"Hush," Evanna stopped me. "I will reveal all shortly. But now it is time for us to move on." She pointed to where the sun was setting on the horizon. "The nights are colder in this time than in yours. We will be safer underground. Besides," she said, rising, "we have an appointment to keep."

"With who?" I asked.

She looked at me steadily. "Our father."

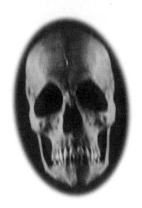

CHAPTER FIFTEEN

Mr. TINY WAS THE LAST person in the world — in all of time! — that I wanted to see. I argued with Evanna hotly, wanting to know why I should present myself to him, or what it could achieve. I hated and feared the meddler more than ever now that I knew so much about him.

"I want to be on the opposite side of the world to wherever he is!" I cried. "Or in another universe, if possible!"

"I understand," Evanna said, "but we must go to him regardless."

"Is he forcing you to do this?" I asked. "Is he the one who ordered me fished out of the Lake? Is he making you take me to him, so that he can mess my life up all over again?"

"You will find out when you meet him," Evanna

said coolly, and since I didn't really have any option but to follow her lead — she could have had me tossed back into the Lake if I disobeyed — eventually, and with much angry muttering, I reluctantly followed after her as she set off into the arid wilderness.

As we left the warmth of the fire, the dragon flapped its wings and took to the skies. I watched it join the throng of dragons far above me, then lost track of it. When I looked back at Evanna, I saw that she was still staring up at the sky. "I wish we could have gone for a flight," she said, sounding curiously sad.

"On the dragon?" I asked.

"Yes. It has always been a wish of mine to fly on a dragon."

"I could call it back," I suggested.

She shook her head quickly. "This isn't the time for it," she said. "And there are too many of them. The others would see us on its back and attack. I don't think you would be able to control so many, not without more practice. And while I can mask us from them down here, I couldn't up there."

As we continued to walk, I looked around and backward, and my gaze settled on the Little People standing motionless by the Lake. "Why are that bunch here?" I asked.

"This is the age in which our father fishes for the souls of the dead to create his Little People," Evanna said, without looking back or slowing. "He could take them from any time, but it's easier this way, when there is nobody to interfere. He leaves a small band of his helpers here, to fish when he gives the order." She glanced at me. "He could have rescued you much earlier. In the present, only two years have passed. He had the power to remove you from the Lake then, but he wanted to punish you. Your sacrifice threw his plans into disarray. He hates you for that, even though you are his son. That's why he sent me forward to this point in time to help you. In this future, your soul has suffered for countless generations. He wanted you to feel the pain of near-eternal imprisonment, and perhaps even go mad from it, so that you couldn't be saved."

"Nice," I grunted sarcastically. Then my eyes narrowed. "If that's the way he feels, why rescue me at all?"

"That will soon become clear," Evanna said.

We walked a long way from the Lake. The air was turning cold around us as the sun dipped. Evanna was looking for a specific spot, pausing every few seconds to examine the ground, then moving on. Finally she found what she was searching for. She came to a halt, knelt, and breathed softly on the dusty earth. There was a rumbling sound, then the ground split at our feet and the mouth of a tunnel opened up. I could only see a dozen feet down it, but I sensed danger.

"Don't tell me we have to go down there," I muttered.

"This is the way to our father's stronghold," she said.

"It's dark," I stalled.

"I will provide light," she promised, and I saw that both her hands were glowing softly, casting a dim white light a few yards ahead of her. She looked at me seriously. "Stay by my side down there. Don't stray."

"Will Mr. Tiny get me if I do?" I asked.

"Believe it or not, there are worse monsters than our father," she said. "We will be passing some of them. If they get their hands on you, your millennia of torment in the Lake of Souls will seem like a pleasant hour spent on a beach."

I doubted that, but the threat was strong enough to ensure that I kept within a hair's breadth of the witch as she started down the tunnel. It sloped at a fairly constant thirty-degree angle. The floor and walls were smooth and made of what looked like solid rock. But there were shapes moving within the rock, twisted, in-human, elongated shapes, all shadows, claws, teeth, and tendrils. The walls bulged outwards as we passed — the *things* trapped within were reaching for us. But none could break through.

"What are they?" I croaked, sweating from fear as much as the dry heat of the tunnel.

"Creatures of universal chaos," Evanna answered. "I told you about them before — they're the monsters I spoke of. They are kin to our father, though he is not as powerful as them. They are imprisoned by a series of temporal and spatial laws — the laws of the universe that our father and I live by. If we ever break the laws, these creatures will be freed. They will turn the universe into a hell of their own making. All will fall beneath them. They'll invade every time zone and torture every mortal being ever born — forever."

"That's why you were angry when you found out I was Mr. Tiny's son," I said. "You thought he'd broken the laws."

"Yes. I was wrong, but it was a close-run thing. I doubt if even he was sure of his plan's success. When he gave birth to Hibernius and me, we knew of the laws, and we obeyed them. If he was wrong about you — if he'd given you more power than he meant to — you could have unknowingly broken the laws and brought about the ruin of everything we know and love." She looked back at me and grinned. "I bet you never guessed you were that important to the world!"

"No," I said sickly. "And I never wanted to be."

"Don't worry," she said, her smile softening. "You took yourself out of the firing line when you let Steve kill you. You did what Hibernius and I never thought possible — you changed what seemed an inevitable future."

"You mean I prevented the coming of the Lord of the Shadows?" I asked eagerly. "That's why I let him kill me. It was the only way I could see to stop it. I didn't want to be a monster. I couldn't bear the thought of destroying the world. Mr. Tiny said one of us had to be the Lord of the Shadows. But I thought, if both of us were dead . . ."

"You thought right," Evanna said. "Our father had edged the world to a point where there were only two futures. When you killed Steve *and* sacrificed yourself, it opened up dozens of possible futures again. I could not have done it — I would have broken the laws if I'd interfered — but as a human, you were able to."

"So what's happened since I died?" I asked. "You said two years have passed. Did the vampires defeat the vampaneze and win the War of the Scars?"

"No," Evanna said, pursing her lips. "The war still rages. But an end is within sight — an end very much not to our father's liking. Persuasive leaders are pushing for peace, Vancha and Harkat Mulds on the side of the vampires, Gannen Harst for the vampaneze. They are debating a treaty, discussing the guidelines by which both sides can live as one. Others fight against them — there are many in both clans who did not wish for peace — but the voices of reason are winning out."

"Then it worked!" I gasped. "If the vampires and vampaneze make peace, the world will be saved!"

"Perhaps," Evanna hummed. "It's not as clear-cut as that. Under Steve, the vampaneze made contact with human political and military leaders. They promised them long lives and power in exchange for their help. They wanted to create nuclear and chemical warfare, with the aim of bringing the world and its survivors under their direct control. That could still happen."

"Then we've got to stop it!" I shouted. "We can't let —"

"Easy," Evanna hushed me. "We are trying to prevent it. That's why I am here. I cannot meddle too deeply in the affairs of mankind, but I can do more now than before, and your actions have convinced me that I *should* interfere. Hibernius and I always stayed neutral. We did not get involved in the affairs of mortals. Hibernius wished to, but I argued against it, afraid we might break the laws and free the monsters." She sighed. "I was wrong. It's necessary to take risks every now and then. Our father took a risk in his attempt to wreak havoc — and I must now take one in an attempt to secure peace."

"What are you talking about?" I frowned.

"Mankind has been evolving," she said. "It has a destiny of its own, a growth toward something wonderful, which our father is intent on ruining. He used the vampires and vampaneze to throw mankind off course, to reduce the cities of the world to rubble, to drag humans back into the dark ages, so that he could control them again. But his plan failed. The clans of the night now seek to reunite and live separately from mankind, hidden, doing no harm, as they did in the past.

"Because the vampires and vampaneze have become part of the present, our father cannot unmake them. He could return to the past and create another race to combat them, but that would be difficult and time-consuming. Time, for once, is against him. If he cannot divide the clans within the next year or so, it is unlikely that he will be able to bring about the downfall of mankind that he craved. He might — and no doubt will — plot afresh in the future, and seek some other way to break them, but for the time being the world will be safe."

Evanna paused. Her hands were directed toward her face, illuminating her features. I'd never seen her look so thoughtful. "Do you remember the story of how I was created?" she asked.

"Of course," I said. "A vampire — Corza Jarn — wanted vampires to be able to have children. He pursued Mr. Tiny until he agreed to grant him his wish, and by mixing Corza Jarn's blood with a pregnant she-wolf, and using his magic on her, he fathered you and Mr. Tall."

"That was not his only reason for creating us," Evanna said, "but it was an important one. I can bear a vampire or a vampaneze's children, and they in turn could have children of their own. But any children of mine will be different from their fathers. They will have some of my powers — not all — and they'll be able to live by day. Sunlight won't kill them."

She looked at me intently. "A new breed of creature, an advanced race of vampire or vampaneze. If I gave birth to such children now, it would drive the clans apart. The warmongers of both sides would use the children to stir up new visions and violence. For instance, if I had a child by a vampire father, those vampires opposed to peace would hail the child as a savior, and say he was sent to help them wipe out the vampaneze. Even if the wiser vampires prevailed, and talked down the troublemakers, the vampaneze would be afraid of the child and suspicious of the vampire clan's long-term plans. How could they discuss peace terms, knowing they were now inferior to vampires, forever at risk?

"The War of the Scars promises to end because both sides see that it might go on forever. When the Lord of the Vampaneze and the vampire hunters were active, everybody knew the war would have a destined end. Now that Steve and you are dead, it might never finish, and neither vampires nor vampaneze want that. So they're willing to talk about peace.

"But my children could change everything. With the renewed promise of victory — either for the vampires or vampaneze, depending on which I chose to be the fathers of my young — the war would continue. As my children grew — and they'd grow quickly, since they'd be creatures of a certain amount of magic — they'd be raised on hatred and fear. In time they'd become warriors and lead their clan to victory over the other — and our father's plan would fall back into place, a little later than anticipated, but otherwise intact."

"Then you mustn't have them!" I exclaimed. "Mr. Tiny can't make you, can he?"

"Not directly," she said. "He has threatened and bribed me ever since the night you and Steve died. But he does not have the power to force me to give birth."

"Then it's OK." I smiled weakly. "You won't have any children, and that will be that."

"Oh, but I will," Evanna said, and lowered her hands so that they shone on her stomach. "In fact, I'm pregnant already."

"*What?*" I exploded. "But you just said —"

"I know."

"But if you —"

"I know."

"But —"

"Darren!" she snapped. "I. Know."

"Then why do it?" I cried.

Evanna stopped to explain. As soon as she paused, the shapes in the walls began to press closer toward us, hissing and snarling, claws and tendrils extending, stretching the fabric of the rock. Evanna spotted this and strode forward again, speaking as she walked.

"I asked Desmond to free your spirit. Guilt drove you to the Lake of Souls, and would have kept you there eternally — there is no natural escape from that Lake of the damned. But rescue is possible. Souls can be fished out. Knowing that you were my half-brother, I felt honor-bound to free you."

"What about Steve?" I asked. "He was your half-brother too."

"Steve deserves his imprisonment." Her eyes were hard. "I feel pity for him, since he was to some extent a victim of our father's meddling. But Steve's evil was primarily of his own making. He chose his path and now must suffer the consequences. But you tried to do good. It wasn't fair that you should rot in the Lake of Souls, so I pleaded with our father to help." She chuckled. "Needless to say, he refused.

"He came to me a few months ago," she continued. "He realized his plans were unraveling and he saw me as his only solution. He'd spent most of the time since your death trying to convince me to have children, with no more success than I'd had trying to get him to free you. But this time he took a fresh approach. He said we could help each other. If I had a child, he'd free your soul."

"You agreed to that?" I roared. "You sold out the world just to help me?"

"Of course not," she grunted.

"But you said you were pregnant."

"I am." She looked back at me and smiled shyly. "My first thought was to reject our father's offer. But then I saw a way to use it to our advantage. There is still no guarantee of a peaceful settlement between the vampires and vampaneze. It looks promising but is by no means certain. If talks break down, the war could continue, and that would play into our father's hands. He would have time to go back to the past and create a new leader, one who could pick up where Steve left off.

"I was thinking of this when Desmond put his suggestion to me. I recalled the way you tricked him, and wondered what you would do in my situation. Then, in a flash, I saw it.

"I accepted his proposal but told him I wasn't sure whether I wanted a vampire's child or a vampaneze's. He said it didn't matter. I asked if I could choose. He said yes. So I spent some time with Gannen Harst, then with Vancha March. When I returned to our father, I told him I had chosen and was pregnant. He was so delighted, he didn't even complain when I refused to reveal who the father was — he just quickly arranged to send me here to free you, so that we could move forward without any further distractions."

She stopped talking and rubbed her stomach with her hands. She was still smiling that strange shy smile.

"So whose is it?" I asked. I didn't see what difference it made but I was curious to know the answer.

"Both," she said. "I am having twins — one by Vancha, one by Gannen."

"A vampire child *and* a vampaneze child!" I cried, excited.

"More than that," Evanna said. "I have allowed

the three bloodlines to mix. Each child is one-third vampire, one-third vampaneze, and one-third me. That's how I've tricked him. He thought any baby of mine would divide the clans, but instead they will pull them closer together. My children, when they are ready, will breed with other vampires and vampaneze, to give birth to a new, multi-race clan. All divisions will be erased and finally forgotten.

"We're going to create peace, Darren, in spite of our father. That's what you taught me — we don't have to accept destiny, *or* Des Tiny. We can create our own future, all of us. We have the power to rule our lives — we just have to make the choice to use it. You chose when you sacrificed your life. Now I've chosen too — by giving life. Only time will tell what our choices lead to, but I'm sure that whatever future we help usher in, it has to be better than the one our father planned."

"Amen to that!" I muttered, then followed her silently down the tunnel, thinking of the future and all the surprises and twists it might hold. My head was buzzing with thoughts and ideas. I was having to take on board so much, so quickly, that I felt overwhelmed by it all, not sure what to make of everything. But there was one thing I was absolutely sure of — when

Mr. Tiny found out about Evanna's babies, he'd all but explode with anger!

Thinking of that, and the nasty little meddler's face when he heard the news, I burst out laughing. Evanna laughed too, and the laughter stayed with us for ages, following us down the tunnel like a flock of chuckling birds, acting almost like a protective spell against the banks of walled-in, ever-moving, ever-reaching monsters.

CHAPTER SIXTEEN

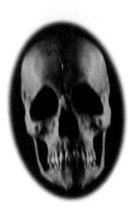

ABOUT AN HOUR LATER the tunnel ended and we entered the home of Desmond Tiny. I'd never really thought of him having a home. I just assumed he wandered the world, always on the move, in search of bloodshed and chaos. But, now that I considered it, I realized every monster needs a den to call its own, and Mr. Tiny's had to be the strangest of them all.

It was a huge — and I mean HUGE — cave, maybe a couple of miles or so wide, and stretching as far ahead as I could make out. Much of the cave was natural, stalagmites and stalactites, waterfalls, beautifully weird rock colors and formations. But much more of it was incredibly *un*natural.

There were grand old cars from what I guessed must be the 1920s or 1930s floating in the air overhead. At first I thought they were attached to the ceiling by wires, but they were in constant motion, circling, crossing paths, even looping around like planes, and not a wire in sight.

There were mannequins all over the place, dressed in costumes from every century and continent, from a primitive loincloth to the most outrageous modern fashion accessories. Their blank eyes unsettled me — I got the feeling that they were watching me, ready to spring to life at Mr. Tiny's command and leap upon me.

There were works of art and sculpture, some so famous that even an art cretin like me recognized them — the *Mona Lisa, The Thinker, The Last Supper.* Mixed in with them, displayed like art exhibits, were dozens of brains preserved in glass cases. I read a few of the labels — Beethoven, Mozart, Wagner, Mahler. (That one gave me a jump — I'd gone to a school named after Mahler!)

"Our father loves music," Evanna whispered. "Where humans collect sheet music or gramophone records —" She obviously hadn't heard about CDs yet! "— he collects brains of composers. By touching them, he can listen to all the tunes they ever composed, along with many they never completed or shared with the world."

"But where does he get them from?" I asked.

"He travels to the past when they have just died

and robs their graves," she said, as though it was the most casual thing in the world. I thought about questioning the right and wrong of something like that, but there were weightier issues to deal with, so I let it slide.

"He likes art too, I take it," I said, nodding at a flowery van Gogh.

"Immensely," Evanna said. "These are all originals, of course — he doesn't bother with copies."

"Nonsense!" I snorted. "These can't be real. I've seen some of the real paintings. Mom and Dad" — I still thought of my human Dad as my real father, and always would — "took me to see the *Mona Lisa* in the Loo once."

"The Louvre," Evanna corrected me. "That is a copy. Some of our father's Little People are created from the souls of artists. They make perfect copies of pieces he especially admires. Then he slips back to the past and swaps the copy for the original. In most cases even the actual artist cannot tell the difference."

"You're telling me the *Mona Lisa* in Paris is a fake?" I asked skeptically.

"Yes." Evanna laughed at my expression. "Our father is a selfish man. He always keeps the best for himself. What he wants, he takes — and he normally wants the best of everything. Except books." Her voice became pointed, as it had earlier when she'd been talking about his attitude toward books. "Desmond never reads works of fiction. He doesn't collect books or pay any attention to authors. Homer, Chaucer, Shakespeare, Dickens, Tolstoy, Twain — all have passed him by unmarked. He doesn't care what they have to say. He has nothing to do with the world of literature. It's as if it exists in a separate universe from his."

Once again I didn't see her point in telling me this, so I let my interest wander. I'd never been a big art fan, but even I was impressed by this display. It was the ultimate collection, capturing a slice of pretty much all the artistic wonder and imagination mankind had ever conjured into being.

There was far too much for any one person to take in. Weapons, jewelry, toys, tools, albums of stamps, bottles of vintage wine, Fabergé eggs, grandfather clocks, suites of furniture, thrones of kings and queens. A lot of it was precious, but there were plenty of worthless items too, stuff that had simply caught Mr. Tiny's fancy, such as bottle tops, oddly shaped balloons, digital watches, a collection of empty ice-cream tubs, thousands of whistles, hundreds of thousands of coins (old ones mixed in with brand-new ones), and so on. The treasure cave in *Aladdin* seemed like a bargain bin in comparison.

Even though the cave was packed with all manner

of wonders and oddities, it didn't feel cluttered. There was plenty of space to walk around and explore. We wound our way through the various collections and artifacts, Evanna pausing occasionally to point out a particularly interesting piece — the charred stake on which Joan of Arc was burnt, the pistol that had been used to shoot Lincoln, the very first wheel.

"Historians would go crazy in this place," I noted. "Does Mr. Tiny ever bring anybody here?"

"Almost never," Evanna said. "This is his private sanctuary. I've only been here a handful of times myself. The exceptions are those he pulls out of the Lake of Souls. He has to bring them here to turn them into Little People."

I stopped when she said that. I'd had a sudden premonition. "Evanna . . ." I began, but she shook her head.

"Ask no more questions," she said. "Desmond will explain the rest to you. It won't be long now."

Minutes later we reached what felt like the center of the cave. There was a small pool of green liquid, a pile of blue robes, and, standing beside them, Mr. Tiny. He was staring at me sourly through the lenses of his thick glasses.

"Well, well," he drawled, hooking his thumbs behind his braces. "If it isn't the young martyr himself. Meet anyone interesting in the Lake of Souls?"

"Ignore him," Evanna said out of the side of her mouth.

Mr. Tiny waddled forward and stopped a few yards shy of me. His eyes seemed to dance with fire this close up. "If I'd known what a nuisance you were going to be, I'd never have spawned you," he hissed.

"Too late now," I jeered.

"No it isn't," he said. "I could go back and erase you from the past, make it so you never lived. The universe would replace you. Somebody else would become the youngest-ever Vampire Prince, hunt for the Vampaneze Lord, et cetera — but *you* would never have existed. Your soul wouldn't just be destroyed — it would be unmade completely."

"Father," Evanna said warningly, "you know you aren't going to do that."

"But I could!" Mr. Tiny insisted.

"Yes," she tutted, "but you won't. We have an agreement. I've upheld my end. Now it's your turn."

Mr. Tiny muttered something unpleasant, then forced a fake smile. "Very well. I'm a man of my word. Let's get on with it. Darren, my woebegotten boy, get rid of that blanket and hop into the pool." He nodded at the green liquid.

"Why?" I asked stiffly.

"It's time to recast you."

A few minutes earlier, I wouldn't have known what he was talking about. But Evanna's hint had prepared me for this. "You want to turn me into a Little Person, don't you?" I said.

Mr. Tiny's lips twitched. He glared at Evanna, but she shrugged innocently. "A perfect little know-it-all, aren't you?" he huffed, disgusted that I'd ruined his big surprise.

"How does it work?" I asked.

Mr. Tiny crossed to the pool and crouched beside it. "This is the soup of creation," he said, running a finger through the thick green liquid. "It will become your blood, the fuel on which your new body runs. Your bones will be stripped bare when you step in. Your flesh, brain, organs, and soul will dissolve. I shall mix it all up and build a new body out of the mess." He grinned, "Those who've been through it tell me it's a most terribly painful procedure, the worst they've ever known."

"What makes you think I'm going to do it?" I asked tightly. "I've seen how your Little People live, mindless, speechless, unable to remember their original identities, slaves to your whims, eating the flesh of dead animals — even humans! Why should I place myself under your spell like that?"

"No deal with my daughter if you don't," Mr. Tiny said simply.

I shook my head stubbornly. I knew Evanna was trying to outfox Mr. Tiny, but I didn't see why this was necessary. How could I help bring about peace between the vampires and vampaneze by going through a load of pain and becoming a Little Person? It didn't make sense.

As if reading my thoughts, Evanna said softly, "This is for *you*, Darren. It has nothing to do with what is happening in the present, or the War of the Scars. This is your only hope of escaping the pull of the Lake of Souls and going to Paradise. You can live a full life as you are, in this waste world, and return to the Lake when you die. Or you can trust us and place yourself in our father's hands."

"I trust *you*," I said to Evanna, shooting an arch look at Mr. Tiny.

"Oh, my boy, if you only knew how much that hurts," Mr. Tiny said miserably, then laughed. "Enough of the dawdling. You either do this or you don't. But take heed, daughter — by making the offer, I've fulfilled my end of the bargain. If the boy refuses to accept your advice it'll be on his head. I'll expect you to keep your word."

Evanna looked at me questioningly, not placing any pressure on me. I thought about it at length. I hated the idea of becoming a Little Person. It wasn't so much the pain as letting Mr. Tiny become my master.

And what if Evanna was lying? I'd said I trusted the witch, but thinking back, I realized there was precious little reason to trust her. She'd never betrayed her father before, or worked for the good of any individual. Why start now? What if this was a twisted scheme to ensnare me, and she was in league with Mr. Tiny, or had been tricked into doing his bidding? The whole thing stank of a trap.

But what other option did I have? Give Evanna the cold shoulder, refuse to enter the pool, walk away? Even assuming Mr. Tiny let me leave, and the monsters in the tunnel didn't catch me, what would I have to look forward to? A life lived in a world full of dragons, followed by eternity in the Lake of Souls, wasn't my idea of a good time! In the end I decided it was better to gamble and hope for the best.

"OK," I said reluctantly. "But there's one condition."

"You're in no position to set conditions," Mr. Tiny growled.

"Maybe not," I agreed, "but I'm setting one anyway. I'll only do it if you guarantee me a free memory. I don't want to wind up like Harkat, not knowing who I was, obeying your orders because I have no free will of my own. I'm not sure what you have planned for me once I become a Little Person, but if it involves serving as one of your fog-brained slaves . . ."

"It doesn't," Mr. Tiny interrupted. "I admit I quite like the idea of having you toady to me for a few million years or so, but my daughter was very precise when it came to the terms of our agreement. You won't be able to talk, but that's the only restriction."

"Why won't I be able to talk?" I frowned.

"Because I'm sick of listening to you!" Mr. Tiny barked. "Besides, you won't need to speak. Most of my Little People don't. Muteness hasn't harmed any of the others, and it won't harm you."

"OK," I muttered. I didn't like it, but I could see there was no point arguing. Stepping up to the edge of the pool, I shrugged off the blanket that the Little People had draped around me shortly after I emerged from the Lake of Souls. I stared into the dark green liquid. I couldn't see my reflection in it. "What —" I started to ask.

"No time for questions!" Mr. Tiny barked and nudged me hard with an elbow. I teetered on the edge of the pool a moment, arms flailing, then splashed heavily into what felt like the sizzling fires of hell.

CHAPTER SEVENTEEN

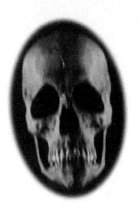

Instant agony and burning. My flesh bubbled, then boiled away. I tried to scream, but my lips and tongue had already come undone. My eyes and ears melted. No sensation except pain.

The liquid stripped my flesh from my bones, then set to work on the marrow within the bones. Next it burned through to my inner organs, then ate me up from the inside out. Inside my head my brain sizzled like a slab of butter in a heated frying pan, and melted down just as quickly. My left arm — just bone now — tore loose from my body and floated away. It was soon followed by my lower right leg. Then I came apart completely, limbs, charred organs, tiny strips of flesh, bare pieces of bone. All that stayed constant was the pain, which hadn't lessened in the slightest.

In the midst of my suffering came a moment of

spiritual calm. With whatever remained of my brain, I became aware of a separation. There was another presence in the pool with me. At first I was confused, but then I realized it was the flicker of Sam Grest's soul which I'd carried within me since drinking his blood at the time of his death. Sam had passed on to Paradise many years ago, and now this final shard of his spirit was departing this world too. In my mind's eye a face formed in the liquid, young and carefree, smiling in spite of the torment, popping a pickled onion into his mouth. Sam winked at me. A ghostly hand saluted. Then he was gone and I was finally, totally alone.

Eventually the pain ceased. I'd dissolved completely. There were no pain sensors left to transmit feelings, and no brain cells to respond to them. A weird peace descended. I'd become one with the pool. My atoms had mixed with the liquid and the two were now one. I *was* the green liquid. I could sense the hollow bones from my body drifting to the bottom of the pool, where they settled.

Some time later, hands — Mr. Tiny's — were dunked in the liquid. He wiggled his fingers, and a shiver ran up the memory of my spine. He picked up the bones from the floor — being careful to scrape up every single piece — and dumped them on the ground of the cave. The bones were covered in molecules of the liquid —

molecules of *me* — and through them I felt Mr. Tiny putting the bones together, snapping them into small pieces, melting some down, bending or twisting others, creating a frame entirely different to my previous form.

Mr. Tiny worked on the body for hours. When he had all the bones in place, he packed them full with organs — brain, heart, liver, kidneys — then covered them with clammy grey flesh, which he stitched together to hold the organs and bones in place. I'm not sure where the organs and flesh came from. Perhaps he grew them himself, but I think it more likely that he harvested them from other creatures — probably dead humans.

Mr. Tiny finished with the eyes. I could feel him connecting the orbs up to my brain, fingers working at lightning-fast speed, with all the precision of the world's greatest surgeon. It was an incredibly artistic under-taking, one which even Dr. Frankenstein would have struggled to match.

Once he finished with the body, he stuck his fingers back into the liquid of the pool. The fingers were cold this time, and grew colder by the second. The liquid be-gan to condense, becoming thicker. There was no pain. It was just strange, like I was squeezing in upon myself.

Then, when the liquid was a fraction of the size it had been, with the texture of a thick milk shake, Mr. Tiny removed his hands and inserted tubes. There was a brief pause, then suction from the tubes, and I felt myself flowing through them, out of the pool and into . . . what? . . . not tubes like those that had been stuck into the pool, but similar. . . .

Of course — *veins*! Mr. Tiny had told me the liquid would serve as my fuel — my blood. I was leaving the confines of the pool for the fleshy limits of my new body.

I felt myself fill the gaps, forcing my way through the network of veins and arteries, making slow but sure progress. When the liquid hit the brain and gradually seeped into it, absorbed by the cold grey cells, my bodily senses awoke. I became aware of my heartbeat first, slower and heavier than before. A tingle ran through my hands and feet, then up my newly crafted spine. I twitched my fingers and toes. Moved an arm slightly. Shook a leg softly. The limbs didn't respond as quickly as my old limbs had, but maybe that was just because I wasn't used to them yet.

Sound came next, a harsh roaring noise at first, which gradually died away to allow normal sounds through. But the sounds weren't as sharp as before — like all the Little People, my ears had been stitched within the skin of my head. Hearing was soon followed by a dim sense of vision — but no smell or sense or taste, since — again, in common with all of Mr. Tiny's creations — I'd been created without a nose.

My vision improved as more and more blood was transferred to my new brain. The world looked different through these eyes. I had a wider field of view than before, since my eyes were rounder and bigger. I could see more, but through a slightly green haze, as though staring through a filter.

The first sight I fixed on was Mr. Tiny, still working on my body, monitoring the tubes, applying a few final stitches, testing my reflexes. He had the look of a loving, devoted parent.

Next I saw Evanna, keeping a close eye on her father, making sure he didn't pull any tricks. She handed him needles and string from time to time, like a nurse. Her expression was a mixture of suspicion and pride. Evanna knew all of Mr. Tiny's shortcomings, but she was still his daughter, and I could see now that despite her misgivings she loved him — in a way.

Eventually the transfer was complete. Mr. Tiny removed the tubes — they'd been stuck in all over, my arms, legs, torso, head — and sealed the holes, stitching them shut. He gave me a final once-over, fixed a spot where I was leaking, did some fine-tuning at the corners of my eyes, checked my heartbeat. Then he stepped back and grunted. "Another perfect creation, even if I do say so myself."

"Sit up, Darren," Evanna said. "But slowly. Don't rush."

I did as she said. A wave of dizziness swept over me when I raised my head, but it soon passed. I pushed up gradually, pausing every time I felt dizzy or sick. Finally I was sitting upright. I was able to study my body from here, its broad hands and feet, thick limbs, dull grey skin. I noted that, like Harkat, I was neither fully male nor female, but something in between. If I could have blushed, I would have!

"Stand," Mr. Tiny said, spitting on his hands and rubbing them together, using his spit to wash himself. "Walk around. Test yourself. It won't take you long to get used to your new shape. I design my Little People to go into immediate action."

With Evanna's help I stood. I weaved unsteadily on my feet but soon found my balance. I was much stouter and heavier than before. As I'd noticed when lying down, my limbs didn't react as quickly as they once did. I had to focus hard to make my fingers curl or to edge a foot forward.

"Easy," Evanna said as I tried to turn and almost fell back into the now-empty pool. She caught and held me until I was steady again. "Slowly, a little bit at

a time. It won't take long — just five or ten minutes."
I tried to ask a question, but no sound came out. "You
cannot speak," Evanna reminded me. "You do not
have a tongue."

I slowly raised a chunky grey arm and pointed a
finger at my head. I stared at Evanna with my large
green eyes, trying to transmit my question mentally.
"You want to know if we can communicate telepathi-
cally," Evanna said. I nodded my neckless head. "No.
You have not been designed with that ability.

"You're a basic model," Mr. Tiny chipped in. "You
won't be around very long, so it would have been
pointless to equip you with a bunch of unnecessary
features. You can think and move, which is all you
need to do."

I spent the next several minutes getting to know
my new body. There were no mirrors nearby, but I
spotted a large silver tray in which I could study my
reflection. Hobbling over to it, I ran a critical green
eye over myself. I was maybe four and a half feet tall
and three feet wide. My stitches weren't as neat as
Harkat's, and my eyes weren't exactly level, but otherwise we didn't look too different. When I opened my
mouth I saw that I lacked not only a tongue, but teeth
too. I turned carefully and looked at Evanna, pointing
to my gums.

"You will not have to eat," she said.

"You won't be alive long enough to bother with food," Mr. Tiny added.

My new stomach clenched when he said that. I'd been tricked! It *had* been a trap, and I'd fallen for it! If I could have spoken, I'd have cursed myself for being such a fool.

But then, as I looked for a decent weapon to defend myself with, Evanna smiled positively. "Remember why we did this, Darren — to free your soul. We could have given you a new, full life as a Little Person, but that would have complicated matters. It's easier this way. You have to trust us."

I didn't feel very trusting, but the deed was done. And Evanna didn't look like somebody who'd been tricked, or who was gloating from having tricked me. Putting fears of betrayal and thoughts of fighting aside, I decided to stay calm and see what the pair planned next for me.

Evanna picked up the pile of blue robes that had been lying near the pool and came over with them. "I prepared these for you earlier," she said. "Let me help you put them on." I was going to signal that I could dress myself, but Evanna flashed me a look that made me stop. Her back was to Mr. Tiny, who was examining the remains of the pool. While his attention was diverted, she slipped the robes on over my head and arms. I realized there were several objects inside the robes, stitched into the lining.

Evanna locked gazes with me and a secret understanding passed between us — she was telling me to act as if the objects weren't there. She was up to something that she didn't want Mr. Tiny to know about. I had no idea what she might have hidden in the robes, but it must be important. Once the robes were on I kept my arms out by my sides and tried not to think about the secret packages I was carrying, in case I accidentally tipped off Mr. Tiny.

Evanna gave me a final once-over, then called out, "He is ready, father."

Mr. Tiny waddled across. He looked me up and down, sniffed snootily, then thrust a small mask at me. "You'd better put that on," he said. "You probably won't need it, but better safe than sorry."

As I strapped on the mask, Mr. Tiny bent and drew a line in the earth of the cave floor. He stepped back from it and clutched his heart-shaped watch. The timepiece began to glow, and soon his hand and face were glowing too. Moments later a doorway grew out of the line in the ground, sliding upward to its full height. It was an open doorway. The space between the jambs was a grey sheen. I'd been through a portal like this before, when Mr. Tiny had sent Harkat and me into what would have been the future (what still might be, if Evanna's plan failed).

When the doorway was complete, Mr. Tiny nodded his head at it. "Time to go."

My eyes flicked to Evanna — was she coming with me? "No," she said in answer to my unasked question. "I will return to the present through a separate door. This one goes further back." She stooped so we were at the same height. "This is good-bye, Darren. I don't imagine I'll ever make the journey to Paradise — I don't think it's intended for the likes of me — so we'll probably never see each other again."

"Maybe he won't go to Paradise either," Mr. Tiny sneered. "Perhaps his soul is meant for the great fires beneath."

Evanna smiled. "We don't know all the secrets of the beyond, but we've never seen any evidence of a hell. The Lake of Souls seems to be the only place where the damned end up, and if our plan works, you won't go back there. Don't worry — your soul will fly free."

"Come on," Mr. Tiny snapped. "I'm bored with him. Time to kick him out of our lives, once and for all." He pushed Evanna aside, grabbed the shoulder of my robes, and hauled me to the doorway. "Don't get any smart ideas back there," he growled. "You can't change the past, so don't go trying. Just do what you have to — tough luck if you can't work out what that is — and let the universe take care of the rest."

I turned my face toward him, not sure what he meant, wanting more answers. But Mr. Tiny ignored me, raised a boot-clad foot, then — without a word of farewell, as though I was a stranger who meant nothing to him — booted me clean through the door and back to a date with history.

CHAPTER EIGHTEEN

"LADIES AND GENTLEMEN, WELCOME to the Cirque Du Freak, home of the world's most remarkable human beings."

I had no eyelids, so I couldn't blink, but beneath my mask my jaw dropped a hundred miles. I was in the wings of a large theater, staring out at a stage and the unmistakable figure of the dead Hibernius Tall. Except he wasn't dead. He was very much alive, and in the middle of introducing one of the fabled Cirque Du Freak performances.

"We present acts both frightening and bizarre, acts you can find nowhere else in the world. Those who are easily scared should leave now. I'm sure there are people who . . ."

Two beautiful women stepped up next to me and prepared to go on. They were tugging at their glittering costumes, making sure they fit right. I recognized the women — Davina and Shirley. They'd been part of the Cirque Du Freak when I first joined, but had left after a few years to get jobs in the ordinary world. The life of a traveling performer wasn't for everyone.

". . . is unique. And none are harmless," Mr. Tall finished, then walked off. Davina and Shirley moved forward and I saw where they were heading — the Wolf Man's cage, which stood uncovered in the middle of the stage. As they left, a Little Person took his place by my side. His face was hidden beneath the hood of his blue robes, but his head turned in my direction. There was a moment's pause, then he reached up and pulled my hood further over my face, so that my features were hidden too.

Mr. Tall appeared by our side with the speed and silence for which he was once renowned. Without a word he handed each of us a needle and lots of orange string. The other Little Person stuck the needle and string inside his robes, so I did the same, not wanting to appear out of place.

Davina and Shirley had released the Wolf Man from his cage and were walking through the audience with him, letting people stroke the hairy man-beast. I studied the theater more closely while they paraded the Wolf Man around. This was the old abandoned movie theater in my hometown, where Steve had murdered Shancus, and where — many years earlier — I had first crossed paths with Mr. Crepsley.

I was wondering why I'd been sent back here — I had a pretty good hunch — when there was a loud explosion. The Wolf Man went wild, as he often did at the start of an act — what looked like a mad outburst was actually carefully staged. Leaping on a screaming woman, he bit one of her hands off. In a flash, Mr. Tall had left our side and reappeared next to the Wolf Man. He pulled him off the screaming woman, subdued him, then led him back to his cage, while Davina and Shirley did their best to calm down the crowd.

Mr. Tall returned to the screaming woman, picked up her severed hand and whistled loudly. That was the signal for my fellow Little Person and me to advance. We ran over to Mr. Tall, careful not to reveal our faces. Mr. Tall sat the woman up and whispered to her. When she was quiet he sprinkled a sparkly pink powder onto her bleeding wrist and stuck the hand against it. He nodded to my companion and me. We pulled out our needles and string and started to stitch the hand back onto the wrist.

I felt light-headed while I stitched. This was the greatest sense of déjà vu I'd ever experienced! I knew what was coming next, every second of it. I'd been sent back into my past, to a night that had been etched unforgettably into my memory. All the times I'd prayed for the chance to come back and change the course of my future. And now, in the most unexpected of circumstances, here it was.

We finished stitching and returned backstage. I wanted to stand in the shadows again and watch the show — if I remembered correctly, Alexander Ribs would come on next, followed by Rhamus Twobellies — but my fellow Little Person was having none of it. He nudged me ahead of him, to the rear of the theater, where a young Jekkus Flang was waiting. In later years Jekkus would become an accomplished knife-thrower, and even take part in the shows. But in this time he'd only recently joined the circus, and was in charge of preparing the interval gift trays.

Jekkus handed each of us a tray packed with items such as rubber dolls of Alexander Ribs, clippings of the Wolf Man's hair, and chocolate nuts and bolts. He also gave us price tags for each item. He didn't speak to us — this was back in the time before Harkat Mulds, when everyone thought Little People were mute, mindless robots.

When Rhamus Twobellies stomped offstage, Jekkus sent us out into the audience to sell the gifts. We moved among the crowd, letting people study our wares and buy if they wished. My fellow Little Person took charge of the rear areas of the theater, leaving me to handle the front rows. And so, a few minutes later, as I'd come to suspect I would, I came face to face with two young boys, the only children in the entire theater. One was a child, the sort of kid who stole money from his mother and collected horror comics, who dreamed of being a vampire when he grew up. The other was a quiet, but in his own way equally mischievous boy, the kind who wouldn't think twice about stealing a vampire's spider.

"How much is the glass statue?" the impossibly young and innocent Steve Leopard asked, pointing to an edible statue on my tray. Shakily, fighting to keep my hand steady, I showed him the price tag. "I can't read," Steve said. "Will you tell me how much it costs?"

I noted the look of surprise on Darren's — *Charna's guts!* — on *my* face. Steve had guessed right away that there was something strange about the Little People, but I hadn't been so sharp. The young me had no idea why Steve was lying.

I shook my head quickly and moved on, leaving Steve to explain to my younger self why he'd pretended he couldn't read. If I'd been feeling light-headed earlier, I felt positively empty-headed now. It's a remarkable, earth-shattering thing to look into the eyes of a youthful you, to see yourself as you once were, young, foolish, gullible. I don't think anyone ever remembers what they were really like as kids. Adults think they do, but they don't. Photos and videos don't capture the real you, or bring back to life the person you used to be. You have to return to the past to do that.

We finished selling our wares and headed backstage to collect fresh trays full of new items, based on the next set of performers — Truska, Hans Hands, and then, appearing like a phantom out of the shadows of the night, Mr. Crepsley and his performing tarantula, Madam Octa.

I couldn't miss Mr. Crepsley's act. When Jekkus wasn't looking, I crept forward and watched from the wings. My heart leaped into my mouth when my old friend and mentor walked onto the stage, startling in his red cloak with his white skin, orange crop of hair, and trademark scar. Seeing him again, I wanted to rush out and throw my arms around him, tell him how much I missed him and how much he'd meant to me. I wanted to joke with him about his stiff manner, his stunted sense of humor, his overly precious pride. I wanted to tell him how Steve had tricked him, and gently wind him up for being taken in by the pretense and dying for no reason. I was sure he'd see the funny side of it once he stopped steaming!

But there could be no communication between us.

Even if I'd had a tongue, Mr. Crepsley wouldn't have known who I was. On this night he hadn't yet met the boy named Darren Shan. I was nobody to him.

So I stood where I was and watched. One final turn from the vampire who'd altered my life in so many ways. One last performance to savor, as he put Madam Octa through her paces and thrilled the crowd. I shivered when he first spoke — I'd forgotten how deep his voice was — then hung on his every word. The minutes passed slowly, but not slowly enough for me — I wanted it to last an eternity.

A Little Person led a goat onstage for Madam Octa to kill. It wasn't the Little Person who'd been with me in the audience — there were more than two of us here. Madam Octa killed the goat, then performed a series of tricks with Mr. Crepsley, crawled over his body and face, pulsed in and out of his mouth, played with tiny cups and saucers. In the crowd, the young Darren Shan was falling in love with the spider — he thought she was amazing. In the wings, the older Darren regarded her sadly. I used to hate Madam Octa — I could trace all my troubles back to the eight-legged beast — but not any longer. None of it was her fault. It was destiny. All along, from the first moment of my being, it had been Des Tiny.

Mr. Crepsley concluded his act and left the stage.

He had to pass me to get off. As he approached, I thought again about trying to communicate with him. I wasn't able to speak, but I could write. If I grabbed him and took him aside, scribbled a message, warned him to leave immediately, to get out now . . .

He passed.

I did nothing.

This wasn't the way. Mr. Crepsley had no reason to trust me, and explaining the situation would have taken too much time — he was illiterate, so I'd have had to get somebody to read the note for him. It might also have been dangerous. If I'd told him about the Vampaneze Lord and all the rest, he might have tried to change the course of the future, to prevent the War of the Scars. Evanna had said it was impossible to change the past, but if Mr. Crepsley — prompted by my warning — somehow managed to do so, he might free those terrible monsters that even Mr. Tiny was afraid of. I couldn't take that risk.

"What are you doing here?" someone snapped behind me. It was Jekkus Flang. He poked me hard with a finger and pointed to my tray. "Get out there quick!" he growled.

I did as Jekkus ordered. I wanted to follow the same route as before, so that I could study myself and Steve again, but this time the other Little Person got there before me, so I had to trudge to the rear of the theater and do the rounds there.

At the end of the interval Gertha Teeth took to the stage, to be followed by Sive and Seersa (the Twisting Twins) and finally Evra and his snake. I retreated to the rear of the theater, not thrilled with the idea of seeing Evra again. Although the snake-boy was one of my best friends, I couldn't forget the pain I'd put him through. It would have hurt too much to watch him perform, thinking about the agony and loss he was to later endure.

While the final trio of acts brought the show to a close, I turned my attention to the objects stitched into the lining of my robes. Time to find out what Evanna had sent me back with. Reaching underneath the heavy blue cloth, I found the first of the rectangular items and ripped it loose. When I saw what it was, I broke out into a wide, toothless smile.

The sly old witch! I recalled what she'd told me on the way from the Lake of Souls to Mr. Tiny's cave — although the past couldn't be changed, the people involved in major events could be replaced. Sending me back to this period in time was enough to free my soul, but Evanna had gone one step further, and made sure I was able to free my old self too. Mr. Tiny knew about that. He didn't like it, but he'd accepted it.

However, working on the sly, unknown to her father,

Evanna had presented me with something even more precious than personal freedom — something that would drive Des Tiny absolutely cuckoo when he found out how he'd been swindled!

I pulled all the other objects out, set them in order, then checked the most recent addition. I didn't find what I expected, but as I scanned through it, I saw what Evanna had done. I was tempted to flick to the rear and read the last few words, but then decided I'd be better off not knowing.

I heard screams from within the theater — Evra's snake must have made its first appearance of the night. I didn't have much time left. I slipped away before Jekkus Flang sought me out and burdened me with another tray. Exiting by the back door, I sneaked around and reentered the theater at the front. I walked down the long corridor to where an open door led to a staircase — the way up to the balcony.

I climbed a few steps, then set Evanna's gift down and waited. I thought about what to do with the objects — the *weapons*. Give them to the boy directly? No. If I did, he might use them to try to change the future. That wasn't allowed. But there must be a way to get them to him, later, so that he could use them at the right time. Evanna wouldn't have given them to me if there wasn't.

It didn't take me long to figure it out. I was happier when I knew what to do with the gift, because it also meant I knew exactly what to do with young Darren.

The show ended, and the audience members poured out of the theater, eagerly discussing the show and marveling aloud. Since the boys had been sitting near the front, they were two of the last to leave. I waited in silence, safe in the knowledge of what was to come.

Finally, a frightened young Darren opened the door to the stairway, slipped through, closed it behind him, and stood in the darkness, breathing heavily, heart pounding, waiting for everyone to file out of the theater. I could see him in spite of the gloom — my large green eyes were almost as strong as a half-vampire's — but he had no idea I was there.

When the last sounds had faded, the boy came slouching up the stairs. He was heading for the balcony, to keep an eye on his friend Steve and see that he came to no harm. If he made it up there, his fate would be sealed and he'd have to live the tormented life of a half-vampire. I had the power to change that. This, in addition to freedom from the Lake of Souls, was Evanna's gift to me — and the last part of the gift as far as Mr. Tiny was aware.

As young Darren drew close, I launched myself at him, picked him up before he knew what was happening, and ran with him down the stairs. I burst through the door into the light of the corridor, then dumped him roughly on the floor. His face was a mask of terror.

"D-d-d-don't kill me!" he squealed, scrambling backwards.

In answer I tore my hood back, then ripped off my mask revealing my round, grey, stitched-together face and huge gaping maw of a mouth. I thrust my head forward, leered, and spread my arms. Darren screamed, lurched to his feet, and stumbled for the exit. I pounded after him, making lots of noise, scraping the wall with my fingers. He flew out of the theater when he got to the door, rolled down the steps, then picked himself up and ran for his life.

I stood on the front doorstep, watching my younger self flee for safety. I was smiling softly. I'd stand guard here to be certain, but I was sure he wouldn't return. He'd run straight home, leap beneath the bedcovers, and shiver himself to sleep. In the morning, not having seen what Steve was up to, he'd call to find out if his friend was OK. Not knowing who Mr. Crepsley was, he'd have no reason to fear Steve, and Steve would have no reason to be suspicious of Darren. Their friendship would resume its natural course and, although I was sure they'd talk often about their trip to the Cirque Du Freak, Darren wouldn't go back to steal the spider, and Steve would never reveal the truth about Mr. Crepsley.

I retreated from the entrance and climbed the steps up to the balcony. There, I watched as Steve had his showdown with Mr. Crepsley. He asked to be the vampire's assistant. Mr. Crepsley tested his blood, then rejected him on the grounds that he was evil. Steve left in a rage, swearing revenge on the vampire.

Would Steve still seek out that revenge now that his main nemesis — me — had been removed from the equation? When he grew up, would his path still take him away from normal life and towards the vampaneze? Was he destined to live his life as he had the first time around, only with a different enemy instead of Darren Shan? Or would the universe replace Steve, like me, with somebody else?

I had no way of knowing. Only time would tell, and I wouldn't be around long enough to see the story through to its end. I'd had my innings, and they were just about over. It was time for me to step back, draw a line under my life, and make my final farewell.

But first — one last cunning attempt to wreck the plans of Desmond Tiny!

CHAPTER NINETEEN

THE KEY EVENTS OF THE past can't be changed, but the people in it can. Evanna had told me that if she went back and killed Adolf Hitler, the universe would replace him with somebody else. The major events of World War II would unfold exactly as they were meant to, only with a different figurehead at the helm. This would obviously create a number of temporal discrepancies, but nothing the higher force of the universe couldn't set right.

While I couldn't alter the course of my history, I *could* remove myself from it. Which was what I'd done by scaring off young Darren. The events of my life would unravel the same way they had before. A child would be blooded, travel to Vampire Mountain, unmask Kurda Smahlt, become a Vampire Prince, then hunt for the Vampaneze Lord. But it wouldn't be the boy I'd frightened off tonight. Somebody else — some other child — would have to fill the shoes of Darren Shan.

I felt bad about putting another kid through the tough trials of my life, but at least I knew that in the end — in death — he would be triumphant. The person who replaced me would follow in my footsteps, kill the Vampaneze Lord, and die in the battle, and out of that death peace would hopefully grow. Since the child wouldn't be responsible for his actions, his soul should go straight to Paradise when he died — the universe, I hoped, was harsh but fair.

And maybe it wouldn't even be a boy. Perhaps I'd be replaced by a girl! The new Darren Shan didn't have to be an exact replica of the old one. He or she could come from any background or country. All the child needed was a strong sense of curiosity and a slightly disobedient streak. Anyone with the nerve to sneak out late at night and go see the Cirque Du Freak had the potential to take my place as Mr. Crepsley's assistant.

Since my part would change, the parts of others could change too. Maybe another girl — or boy — would fill Debbie's role, and somebody else could be Sam Grest. Perhaps Gavner Purl wouldn't be the vampire who was killed by Kurda, and even Steve could be replaced by another. Maybe Mr. Crepsley wouldn't be the one to die in the Cavern of Retribution, and would live to be a vampire of ancient years and wisdom, like his mentor, Seba Nile. Many of the parts in the story — the saga — of my life might be up for grabs now that the central character has been changed.

But that was all wild speculation. What I did know for certain was that the boy I'd once been would now lead a normal life. He'd go to school, grow up like anybody else, get a job, maybe raise a family of his own one day. All the things the original Darren Shan had missed out on, the new Darren would enjoy. I'd given him his freedom — his humanity. I could only pray to the gods of the vampires that he made the most of it.

The objects stitched into the lining of my robes were my diaries. I'd kept a diary just about as long as I could remember. I'd recorded everything in it — my trip to the Cirque Du Freak, becoming Mr. Crepsley's assistant, my time in Vampire Mountain, the War of the Scars and hunt for the Vampaneze Lord, right up to that final night when I'd had my fatal last run-in with Steve. It was all there, everything important from my life, along with lots of trivial stuff too.

Evanna had brought the diary up to date. She must have taken it from the house where Debbie and Alice were based, then described all that had happened on that blood-drenched night, the showdown with Steve and my death. She'd then briefly outlined my long years of mental suffering in the Lake of Souls, followed by a more detailed account of my rescue and rebirth as a Little Person. She'd even gone beyond that, and told what happened next, my return, the way I'd scared the original Darren away, and . . .

I don't know what she wrote in the last few pages. I didn't read that far. I'd rather find out for myself what my final actions and thoughts are — not read about them in a book!

After Steve left and Mr. Crepsley retired to the cellar where his coffin was stored, I went in search of Mr. Tall. I found him in his van, going over the night's receipts. He used to do that regularly. I think he enjoyed the normality of the simple task. I knocked on the door and waited for him to answer.

"What do you want?" he asked suspiciously when he saw me. Mr. Tall wasn't used to being surprised, certainly not by a Little Person.

I held the diaries out to him. He looked at them warily, not touching them.

"Is this a message from Desmond?" he asked. I shook my neckless head. "Then what . . . ?" His eyes widened. "No!" he gasped. "It can't be!" He pushed my hood back — I'd replaced it after I'd scared off the young me — and studied my features fiercely.

After a while Mr. Tall's look of concern was replaced by a smile. "Is this my sister's work?" he inquired. I nodded my chunky head a fraction. "I never thought she'd get involved," he murmured. "I imagine there's more to it than just freeing your soul, but I won't press you for information — better for all concerned if I don't know."

I raised the diaries, wanting him to take them, but Mr. Tall still didn't touch them. "I'm not sure I understand," he said.

I pointed to the name — Darren Shan — scrawled across the front of the top copy, then to myself. Opening it, I let him see the date and the first few lines, then flicked forward to where it described my visit to the Cirque Du Freak and what had happened. When he'd read the part where I told about watching Steve from the balcony, I pointed up and shook my head hard.

"Oh," Mr. Tall chuckled. "I see. Evanna not only saved your soul — she gave the old you his normal life back."

I smiled, pleased he finally understood. I closed the

diary, tapped the cover, then offered the books to him again. This time he took them.

"Your plan is clear to me now," he said softly. "You want the world to know of this, but not yet. You are right — to reveal it now would be to risk unleashing the hounds of chaos. But if it's released later, around the time when you died, it could affect only the present and the future."

Mr. Tall's hands moved very swiftly, and the diaries disappeared. "I will keep them safe until the time is right," he said. "Then I will send them to . . . who? An author? A publisher? The person you have become?"

I nodded quickly when he said that.

"Very well," he said. "I cannot say what he will do with these — he might consider them a hoax, or not understand what you want of him — but I'll do as you request." He started to close the door, then paused. "In this time, of course, I do not know you, and now that you have removed yourself from your original time line, I never shall. But I sense we were friends." He put out a hand and we shook. Mr. Tall only very rarely shook hands. "Good luck to you, friend," he whispered. "Good luck to us all." Then he quickly broke contact and closed the door, leaving me to retire, find a nice quiet spot where I could be alone — and die.

———

I now know why Evanna commented on Mr. Tiny not being a reader. He has nothing to do with books. He doesn't pay attention to novels or other works of fiction. If, many years from now, an adult Darren Shan comes along and publishes a series of books about vampires, Mr. Tiny won't know about it. His attention will be focused elsewhere. The books will come out and be read, and even though vampires aren't avid readers, word will surely trickle back to them.

As the War of the Scars comes to a wary pause and leaders on both sides try to forge a new era of peace, my diaries will — with the luck of the vampires—hit bookstores around the world. Vampires and vampaneze will be able to read my story (or have it read to them if they're illiterate). They'll discover more about Mr. Tiny than they ever imagined. They'll see precisely how much of a meddler he really is, and learn of his plans for a desolate future world. Armed with that knowledge, and united by the birth of Evanna's children, I'm certain they'll band together and do all they can to stop him.

Mr. Tall will send my diaries to the grown Darren Shan. I don't imagine he'll add any notes or instructions of his own — he dare not meddle with the past in that way. It's possible the adult me will dismiss the diaries, write them off as a bizarre con job, and do nothing with them. But knowing me the way I do (now *that* sounds weird!), I think, once he's read them, he'll take them at face value. I like to believe I always had an open mind.

If the adult me reads the diaries all the way to the end, and believes they're real, he'll know what to do. Rewrite them, fiddle with the names so as not to draw unwelcome attention to the real people involved, rework the facts into a story, cut out the duller entries, fictionalize it a bit, create an action-packed adventure. And then, when he's done all that — sell it! Find an agent and publisher. Pretend it's a work of fantasy. Get it published. Promote it hard. Sell it to as many countries as he can, to spread the word and increase the chances of the story capturing the attention of vampires and vampaneze.

Am I being realistic? There's a big difference between a diary and a novel. Will the human Darren Shan have the ability to draw readers in and spin a tale which keeps them hooked? Will he be able to write a series of novels strong enough to attract the attention of the children of the night? I don't know. I was pretty good at writing stories when I was younger, but there's no way of knowing what I'll be like when I grow up.

Maybe I won't read anymore. Maybe I won't want to or be able to write.

But I have to hope for the best. Freed from his dark destiny, I have to hope the young me keeps on reading and writing. If the luck of the vampires is really with me (with *us*), maybe that Darren will become a writer even before Mr. Tall sends the package to him. That would be perfect, if he was already an author. He could put the story of my life out as just another of his imaginative works, then get on with writing his own stuff, and nobody — except those actually involved in the War of the Scars — would ever know the difference.

Maybe I'm just dreaming. But it *could* happen. I'm proof that stranger things have taken place. So I say: Go for it, Darren! Follow your dreams. Take your ideas and run with them. Work hard. Learn to write well. I'll be waiting for you up ahead if you do, with the weirdest, twistiest story you've ever heard. Words have the power to alter the future and change the world. I think, together, we can find the right words. I can even, now that I think about it, suggest a first line for the book to start you out on the long and winding road, perhaps something along the lines of, "I've always been fascinated by spiders . . ."

CHAPTER TWENTY

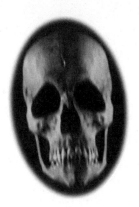

I'M ON THE ROOF of the old movie theater, lying on my back, studying the beautiful sky. Dawn is close. Thin clouds drift slowly across the lightening horizon. I can feel myself coming undone. It won't be much longer now.

I'm not one hundred percent sure how Mr. Tiny's resurrection process works, but I think I understand enough of it to know what's going on. Harkat was created from the remains of Kurda Smahlt. Mr. Tiny took Kurda's corpse and used it to create a Little Person. He then returned Harkat to the past. Harkat and Kurda shouldn't have been able to exist simultaneously. A soul can't normally share two bodies at the same time. One should have given way to the other. As the original, Kurda had the automatic right to life, so Harkat's body should have started to unravel, as it did when

Kurda was fished out of the Lake of Souls all those years later.

But it didn't. Harkat survived for several years in the same time zone as Kurda. That makes me assume that Mr. Tiny has the power to protect his Little People, at least for a while, even if he sends them back to a time when their original forms are still alive.

But he didn't bother to protect *me* when he sent me back. So one of the bodies has to go — this one. But I'm not moaning. I'm OK with my brief spell as a Little Person. In fact, the shortness of this life is the whole point! It's how Evanna has freed me.

When Kurda was facing death for the second time, Mr. Tiny told him that his spirit wouldn't return to the Lake — it would depart this realm. By dying now, my soul — like Kurda's — will fly immediately to Paradise. I suppose it's a bit like not passing "Go" on a Monopoly board and going straight to jail, except in this case "Go" is the Lake of Souls and "jail" is the afterlife.

I feel exceptionally light, as though I weigh almost nothing. The sensation is increasing by the moment. My body's fading away, dissolving. But not like in the green pool of liquid in Mr. Tiny's cave. This is a gentle, painless dissolve, as though some great force is unstitching me, using a pair of magical knitting needles to pick my flesh and bones apart, strand by strand, knot by knot.

What will Paradise be like? I can't answer that one. I can't even hazard a guess. I imagine it's a timeless place, where the dead souls of every age mingle as one, renewing old friendships and making new acquaintances. Space doesn't exist, not even bodies, just thoughts and imagination. But I have no proof of that. It's just what I picture it to be.

I summon what little energy I have left and raise a hand. I can see through the grey flesh now, through the muscles and bones, to the twinkle of the stars beyond. I smile and the corners of my lips continue stretching, off my face, becoming a limitless, endless smile.

My robes sag as the body beneath loses the ability to support them. Atoms rise from me like steam, thin tendrils at first, then a steady stream of shafts that are all the colors of the rainbow, my soul departing from every area of my body at once. The tendrils wrap around one another and shoot upward, bound for the stars and realms beyond.

There's almost nothing left of me now. The robes collapse in on themselves completely. The last traces of my spirit hover above the robes and the roof. I think of my family, Debbie, Mr. Crepsley, Steve, Mr. Tiny, all those I've known, loved, feared, and hated. My last thought, oddly, is of Madam Octa — I wonder if they have spiders in Paradise?

And now it's over. I'm finished with this world. My final few atoms rise at a speed faster than light, leaving the roof, the theater, the town, the world, far, far behind. I'm heading for a new universe, new adventures, a new way of being. Farewell, world! Good-bye, Darren Shan! So long, old friends and allies! This is it! The stars draw me toward them. Explosions of space and time. Breaking through the barriers of the old reality. Coming apart, coming together, moving on. A breath on the lips of the universe. All things, all worlds, all lives. Everything at once and never. Mr. Crepsley waiting. Laughter in the great beyond. I'm going . . . I'm . . . going . . . I'm . . . gone.

THE END

CIRQUE DU FREAK

MAY 8, 1997–JANUARY 9, 2006

Book 1

CIRQUE DU FREAK
THE SAGA OF DARREN SHAN

Darren Shan is just an ordinary schoolboy—until he gets an invitation to visit the Cirque Du Freak. Soon, Darren and his friend Steve are caught in a deadly trap. Darren must make a bargain with the one person who can save Steve. But that person is not human and deals only in blood. . . .

Book 2

CIRQUE DU FREAK The Vampire's Assistant
THE SAGA OF DARREN SHAN

As a vampire's assistant, Darren struggles to resist the one temptation that sickens him—the one thing that can keep him alive. But destiny is calling—the wolf-man is waiting.

Book 3

CIRQUE DU FREAK Tunnels of Blood
THE SAGA OF DARREN SHAN

When corpses are discovered—drained of blood—Darren and Evra are compelled to hunt down whatever foul creature is committing such acts. Beneath the streets, evil stalks. Can they escape, or are they doomed to perish in the tunnels of blood?

Book 4

CIRQUE DU FREAK Vampire Mountain
THE SAGA OF DARREN SHAN

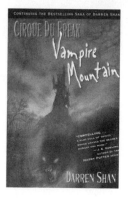

Darren Shan and Mr. Crepsley embark on a dangerous trek to the very heart of the vampire world. Will a meeting with the Vampire Princes restore Darren's human side, or push him further towards the darkness?

Book 5

CIRQUE DU FREAK Trials of Death
THE SAGA OF DARREN SHAN

Darren Shan must pass five fearsome Trials to prove himself to the vampire clan—or face the stakes in the Hall of Death. But Vampire Mountain holds hidden threats. In this nightmarish world of bloodshed and betrayal, death may be a blessing.

Book 6

CIRQUE DU FREAK The Vampire Prince
THE SAGA OF DARREN SHAN

Can Darren, the vampire's assistant, reverse the odds and outwit a Vampire Prince, or is this the end of thousands of years of vampire rule?

Book 7

CIRQUE DU FREAK
THE SAGA OF DARREN SHAN
Hunters of the Dusk

As part of an elite force, Darren searches the world for the Vampaneze Lord. But the road ahead is long and dangerous—and lined with the bodies of the damned.

Book 8

CIRQUE DU FREAK
THE SAGA OF DARREN SHAN
Allies of the Night

Darren Shan, Vampire Prince and vampaneze killer, faces his worst nightmare yet—school! But homework is the least of Darren's problems. Bodies are piling up. Time is running out.

Book 9

CIRQUE DU FREAK
THE SAGA OF DARREN SHAN
Killers of the Dawn

Pursued by the vampaneze, the police, and an angry mob, Darren Shan the Vampire Prince is public enemy number one! With their enemies clamoring for blood, the vampires prepare for a deadly battle. Is this the end for Darren and his allies?

CIRQUE DU FREAK The Lake
THE SAGA OF DARREN SHAN
of Souls

Darren and Harkat face monstrous obstacles on their desperate quest to the Lake of Souls. Will they survive the savage journey? And what awaits them in the murky waters of the dead? Be careful what you fish for. . . .

CIRQUE DU FREAK Lord of
THE SAGA OF DARREN SHAN
the Shadows

Darren Shan is going home—and his world is going to hell. Old enemies await. Scores must be settled. Destiny looks certain to destroy him, and the world is set to fall to the Ruler of the Night. . . .

Grubbs Grady is about to learn three things:
The world is vicious. Magic is possible.
Demons are real.

Turn the page for a sneak peek at Darren Shan's
bloodcurdling new novel:

LORD LOSS

Book 1 in the DEMONATA series

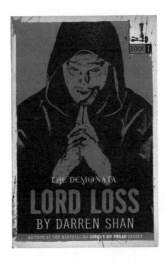

Available now.

✠ Purgatory. Confined to my room after school for a month. A whole bloody *MONTH*! No TV, no computer, no comics, no books — except schoolbooks. Dad leaves my chess set in the room too — no fear my chess-crazy parents would take *that* away from me! Chess is almost a religion in this house. My sister Gret and I were reared on it. While other toddlers were being taught how to put jigsaws together, we were busy learning the ridiculous rules of chess.

I can come downstairs for meals, and bathroom visits are allowed, but otherwise I'm a prisoner. I can't even go out on the weekends.

In solitude, I call Gret every name under the moon the first night. Mom and Dad bear the brunt of my curses the next. After that I'm too miserable to blame anyone, so I sulk in moody silence and play chess against myself to pass the time.

They don't talk to me at meals. The three of them act like I'm not not there. Gret doesn't even glance at me spitefully and sneer, the way she usually does when I'm getting the doghouse treatment.

But what have I done that's so bad? OK, it was a crude joke and I knew I'd get into trouble — but their reactions are waaaaaaay over the top. If I'd done something to embarrass Gret in public, fair enough, I'd take what was coming. But this was a private joke, just between us. They shouldn't be making such a song and dance about it.

Dad's words echo back to me — "And the timing!" I think about them a lot. And Mom's, when she was going on about smoking, just before Dad cut her short — "We don't need this, certainly not at this time, not when —"

What did they mean? What were they talking about? What does the timing have to do with anything?

Something stinks here — and it's not just rat guts.

✠ I spend a lot of time writing. Diary entries, stories, poems. I try drawing a comic — "Grubbs Grady, Superhero!" — but I'm no good at art. I get great marks in my other subjects — way better than goat-faced Gret ever gets, as I often remind her — but I've got all the artistic talent of a duck.

I play lots of games of chess. Mom and Dad are chess fanatics. There's a board in every room and they play several games most nights, against each other or friends from their chess clubs. They make Gret and me play too. My earliest memory is of sucking on a white rook while Dad explained how a knight moves.

I can beat just about anyone my age — I've won regional competitions — but I'm not in the same class as Mom, Dad, or Gret. Gret's won at national level and can wipe the floor with me nine times out of ten. I've only ever beaten Mom twice in my life. Dad — never.

It's been the biggest argument starter all my life. Mom and Dad don't put pressure on me to do well in school or at other games, but they press me all the time at chess. They make me read chess books and watch videotaped tournaments. We have long debates over meals and in Dad's study about legendary games and grandmasters, and how I can improve. They send me to tutors and keep entering me in competitions. I've argued with them about it — I'd rather spend my time watching and playing basketball — but they've always stood firm.

White rook takes black pawn, threatens black queen. Black queen moves to safety. I chase her with my bishop. Black queen moves again — still in danger. This is childish stuff — I could have cut off the threat five moves back, when it became apparent — but I don't care. In a petty way, this is me striking back. "You take my TV and computer away? Stick me up here on my own? OK — I'm gonna learn to play the worst game of chess in the world. See how you like that, Corporal Dad and Commandant Mom!"

Not exactly Luke Skywalker striking back against the evil Empire by blowing up the *Death Star,* I know, but hey, we've all gotta start somewhere!

✠ Studying my hair in the mirror. Stiff, tight, ginger. Dad used to be ginger when he was younger, before the grey set in. Says he was fifteen or sixteen when he noticed the change. So, if I follow in his footsteps, I've only got a handful or so years of unbroken ginger to look forward to.

I like the idea of a few grey hairs, not a whole head of them like Dad, just a few. And spread out — I don't want a skunk patch. I'm big for my age — taller than most of my friends — and burly. I don't look old, but if I had a few grey hairs, I might be able to pass for an adult in poor light — bluff my way into R-rated movies!

The door opens. Gret — smiling shyly. I'm nineteen days into my sentence. Full of hate for Gretelda Grotesque. She's the last person I want to see.

"Get out!"

"I came to make up," she says.

"Too late," I snarl nastily. "I've only got eleven days to go. I'd rather see them out than kiss your . . ." I stop. She's holding out a plastic bag. Something blue inside. "What's that?" I ask suspiciously.

"A present to make up for getting you grounded," she says, and lays it on my bed. She glances out of the window. The curtains are open. A three-quarters moon lights up the sill. There are some chess pieces on it, from when I was playing earlier. Gret shivers, then turns away.

"Mom and Dad said you can come out — the punishment's over. They've ended it early."

She leaves.

Bewildered, I tear open the plastic. Inside — a New York Knicks jersey, shorts and socks. I'm stunned. The Knicks are my team, my basketball champions. Mom used to buy me their latest gear at the start of every season, until I hit puberty and sprouted. She won't buy me any new gear until I stop growing — I outgrew the last one in just a month.

This must have cost Gret a fortune — it's brand new, not last season's. This is the first time she's ever given me a present, except at Christmas and birthdays. And Mom and Dad have never cut short a grounding before — they're very strict about making us stick to any punishment they set.

What the hell is going on?

✠ Three days after my early release. To say things are strange is the understatement of the decade. The atmosphere's just like it was when Grandma died. Mom and Dad wander around like robots, not saying much. Gret mopes in her room or in the kitchen, stuffing herself with sweets and playing chess nonstop. She's like an addict. It's bizarre.

I want to ask them about it, but how? "Mom, Dad — have aliens taken over your bodies? Is somebody dead and you're too afraid to tell me? Have you all converted to Miseryism?"

Seriously, jokes aside, I'm frightened. They're sharing a secret, something bad, and keeping me out of it. Why? Is it to do with me? Do they know something that I don't? Like maybe . . . maybe . . .

(Go on — have the guts! Say it!)

Like maybe *I'm* going to die?

Stupid? An overreaction? Reading too much into it? Perhaps. But they cut short my punishment. Gret gave me a present. They look like they're about to burst into tears at any given minute.

Grubbs Grady — on his way out? A deadly disease I caught on vacation? A brain defect I've had since birth? The big, bad Cancer bug?

What other explanation is there?

✠ "Regale me with your thoughts on ballet."

I'm watching basketball highlights. Alone in the TV room with Dad. I cock my ear at the weird, out-of-nowhere question and shrug. "Rubbish," I snort.

"You don't think it's an incredibly beautiful art form? You've never wished to experience it firsthand? You don't want to glide across Swan Lake or get sweet with a Nutcracker?"

I choke on a laugh. "Is this a windup?"

Dad smiles. "Just wanted to check. I got a great offer on tickets to a performance tomorrow. I bought three — anticipating your less-than-enthusiastic reaction — but I could probably get an extra one if you want to tag along."

"No way!"

"Your loss." Dad clears his throat. "The ballet's out of town and finishes quite late. It will be easier for us to stay in a hotel overnight."

"Does that mean I'll have the house to myself?" I ask excitedly.

"No such luck," he chuckles. "I think you're old enough to guard the fort, but Sharon" — Mom — "has a different view, and she's the boss. You'll have to stay with Aunt Kate."

"Not no-date Kate," I groan. Aunt Kate's only a couple of years older than Mom, but lives like a ninety-year-old. Has a black-and-white TV but only turns it on for the news. Listens to radio the rest of the time. "Couldn't I kill myself instead?" I quip.

"Don't make jokes like that!" Dad snaps with unexpected venom. I stare at him, hurt, and he forces a thin smile. "Sorry. Hard day at the office. I'll arrange it with Kate, then."

He stumbles as he exits — as if he's nervous. For a minute there it was like normal, me and Dad messing around, and I forgot all my recent worries. Now they come flooding back. If I'm not at death's door, why was he so upset at my throwaway gag?

Curious and afraid, I slink to the door and eavesdrop as he phones Aunt Kate and clears my stay with her. Nothing suspicious in their conversation. He doesn't talk about me as if these are my final days. Even hangs up with a cheery "Toodle-oo," a corny phrase he often uses on the phone. I'm about to withdraw and catch up with the basketball action when I hear Gret speaking softly from the stairs.

"He didn't want to come?"

"No," Dad whispers back.

"It's all set?"

"Yes. He'll stay with Kate. It'll just be the three of us."

"Couldn't we wait until next month?"

"Best to do it now — it's too dangerous to put off."

"I'm scared, Dad."

"I know, love. So am I."

Silence.

✠ Mom drops me off at Aunt Kate's. They exchange some small talk on the doorstep, but Mom's in a rush and cuts the conversation short. Says she has to hurry or they'll be late for the ballet. Aunt Kate buys that, but I've cracked their cover story. I don't know what Mom and Co. are up to tonight, but they're not going to watch a load of poseurs in tights jumping around like puppets.

"Be good for your aunt," Mom says, tweaking the hairs on my forehead.

"Enjoy the ballet," I reply, smiling hollowly.

Mom hugs me, then kisses me. I can't remember the last time she kissed me. There's something desperate about it.

"I love you, Grubitsch!" she croaks, almost sobbing.

If I hadn't already known something was very, very wrong, the dread in her voice would have tipped me off. Prepared for it, I'm able to grin and flip back at her, Humphrey Bogart style, "Love you too, shweetheart."

Mom drives away. I think she's crying.

"Make yourself comfy in the living room," Aunt Kate simpers. "I'll fix a nice pot of tea for us. It's almost time for the news."

✠ I make an excuse after the news. Sore stomach — need to rest. Aunt Kate makes me gulp down two large spoons of cod liver oil, then sends me up to bed.

I wait five minutes, until I hear Frank Sinatra crooning — no-date Kate loves Ol' Blue Eyes and always manages to find him on the radio. When I hear her singing along to some corny ballad, I slip downstairs and out the front door.

I don't know what's going on, but now that I know I'm not set to go toes-up, I'm determined to see it through with them. I don't care what sort of a mess they're in. I won't let Mom, Dad, and Gret freeze me out, no matter how bad it is. We're a family. We should face things together. That's what Mom and Dad always taught me.

Padding through the streets, covering the four miles home as quickly as I can. They could be anywhere, but I'll start with the house. If I don't find them there, I'll look for clues to where they might be.

I think of Dad saying he's scared. Mom trembling as she kissed me. Gret's voice when she was on the stairs. My stomach tightens with fear. I ignore it, jog at a steady pace, and try spitting the taste of cod liver oil out of my mouth.

✠ Home. I spot a chink of light in Mom and Dad's bedroom, where the curtains just fail to meet. It doesn't mean they're in — Mom always leaves a light on to deter burglars. I slip around the back and peer through the garage window. The car's parked inside. So they're here. This is where it all kicks off. Whatever "it" is.

I creep up to the back door. Crouch, poke the dog flap open, listen for sounds. None. I was eight when our last dog died. Mom said she was never allowing another one inside the house — they always got killed on the roads and she was sick of burying them. Every few months, Dad says he must board over the dog flap or get a new door, but he never has. I think he's still secretly hoping she'll change her mind. Dad loves dogs.

When I was a baby, I could crawl through the flap. Mom had to keep me tied to the kitchen table to stop me from sneaking out of the house when she wasn't looking. Much too big for it now, so I fish under the pyramid-shaped stone to the left of the door and locate the spare key.

The kitchen's cold. It shouldn't be — the sun's been shining all day and it's a nice warm night — but it's like standing in a refrigerator aisle in a supermarket.

I creep to the hall door and stop, again listening for sounds. None.

Leaving the kitchen, I check the TV room, Mom's fancily decorated living room — off-limits to Gret and me except on special occasions — and Dad's study. Empty. All as cold as the kitchen.

Coming out of the study, I notice something strange and do a double-take. There's a chess board in one corner. Dad's prize chess set. The pieces are based on characters from the King Arthur legends. Hand-carved by some famous craftsman in the nineteenth century. Cost a fortune. Dad never told Mom the exact price — never dared.

I walk to the board. Carved out of marble, four inches thick. I played a game with Dad on its smooth surface just a few weeks ago. Now it's rent with deep, ugly gouges. Almost like fingernail scratches — except no human could drag their nails through solid marble. And all the carefully crafted pieces are missing. The board's bare.

Up the stairs. Sweating nervously. Fingers clenched tight. My breath comes out as mist before my eyes. Part of me wants to turn tail and run. I shouldn't be here. I don't *need* to be here. Nobody would know if I backed up and . . .

I flash back to Gret's face after the rat guts prank. Her tears. Her pain. Her smile when she gave me the Knicks jersey. We fight all the time, but I love her deep down. And not that deep either.

I'm not going to leave her alone with Mom and Dad to face whatever trouble they're in. Like I told myself earlier — we're a family. Dad's always said families should pull together and fight as a team. I want to be part of this — even though I don't know what "this" is, even though Mom and Dad did all they could to keep me out of "this," even though "this" terrifies me senseless.

The landing. Not as cold as downstairs. I try my bedroom, then Gret's. Empty. Very warm. The chess pieces on Gret's board are also missing. Mine haven't been taken, but they lie scattered on the floor and my board has been smashed to splinters.

I edge closer to Mom and Dad's room. I've known all along that this is where they must be. Delaying the moment of truth. Gret likes to call me a coward when she wants to hurt me. Big as I am, I've always gone out of my way to avoid fights. I used to think (*fear*) she might be right. Each step I take towards my parents' bedroom proves to my surprise that she was wrong.

The door feels red hot, as though a fire is burning behind it. I press an ear to the wood — if I hear the crackle of flames, I'll race straight to the phone and dial 911. But there's no crackle. No smoke. Just deep, heavy breathing . . . and a curious dripping sound.

My hand's on the doorknob. My fingers won't move. I keep my ear pressed to the wood, waiting . . . praying. A tear trickles from my left eye. It dries on my cheek from the heat.

Inside the room, somebody giggles — low, throaty, sadistic. Not Mom, Dad, or Gret. There's a ripping sound, followed by snaps and crunches.

My hand turns.

The door opens.

Hell is revealed.

The Demonata exist in a multi-world universe of their own.
Evil, murderous creatures who revel in torment and slaughter.
They try to cross over into our world all the time.

Don't miss Darren Shan's
chilling DEMONATA series.

And watch out for *Bec*,
coming May 2007.